# DEAD MAN TALKING

## AN ALEX MASON THRILLER

### DAVID ARCHER

### BLAKE BANNER

RIGHTHOUSE

ISBN-13: 978-1-63696-308-2

ISBN-10: 1-63696-308-0

Cover design by: Damonza

Printed in the United States of America

www.righthouse.com

www.instagram.com/righthousebooks

www.facebook.com/righthousebooks

twitter.com/righthousebooks

# PRAISE FOR ALEX MASON

"It is brutal, wastes no time, and is full of action."

AMAZON REVIEW

"Better than Bond, Bourne, or Reacher."

AMAZON REVIEW

"For fans of Clancy, Mitch App, and Brad Taylor."

AMAZON REVIEW

"Same level as Patterson or Baldacci."

AMAZON REVIEW

"This book is filled with action, intrigue, espionage, and everything else lovers of a good thriller want."

AMAZON REVIEW

**ALEX MASON THRILLERS**
Odin (Book 1)
Ice Cold Spy (Book 2)
Mason's Law (Book 3)
Assets and Liabilities (Book 4)
Russian Roulette (Book 5)
Executive Order (Book 6)
Dead Man Talking (Book 7)
All The King's Men (Book 8)
Flashpoint (Book 9)
Brotherhood of the Goat (Book 10)
Dead Hot (Book 11)
Blood on Megiddo (Book 12)
Son of Hell (Book 13)

# PROLOGUE

THE DOORBELL RANG AND SAUL SIGHED. SAUL sighed a lot these days. He paused a moment before standing, to look out the open French doors at the glimmering lights of the wet city, five floors below. The wrought iron of the small balcony framed the streetlamps of Church Street. They were glimmering, he thought, not glittering. Glittering was too sparkly. That was New York, Los Angeles, even San Francisco. These lights were softer, wetter, more mellow, like the city. His city. A small smile, as mellow as the lights, touched his eyes. He knew that many thought of him as a traitor, especially in the liberal community, and of his city as a den of corruption and savagery. He didn't accept either. He had betrayed no one, and as for corruption, that was what "They" had done to it. To him this was the home—the source—of everything good and decent and right about humanity.

The doorbell rang again and he sighed again, forced himself to his feet, groaning with middle age, and with his hands on the small of his back, he walked stretching from his cluttered, comfortable office, across his spacious living room to his front door, and opened it.

He frowned and sagged slightly. "I am real busy. This is not a good time."

On receiving no response he turned and walked away from the door, talking over his shoulder as he went. "Fine! Come on in then, but please, make it brief. I lose my thread when I'm distracted..."

He heard the door close softly. Then, "Saul...?" Something in the voice made him stop and turn. He got as far as, "What...?" before the .44 caliber slug punched a half-inch hole into his forehead and a four-inch hole out the back of his head, spraying his considerable brains across the parquet floor and the genuine Persian rug. He went down straight like a tree and hit the floor with a jarring smack.

His visitor smiled. "You always complained of a stiff back. I bet it's never been as stiff as this, has it?"

His visitor then crossed the living room to Saul's study.

# ONE

It was raining on Campden Hill Square. It was not so much heavy as steady, relentless. You got the feeling it could go on like this indefinitely, till long after you had become exhausted and died of old age. There was the steady sound of wet splatter—an overflowing gutter somewhere—and through the open window of my rented Jaguar I could smell damp wooden fenceposts and creosote. It was a very English smell on a very English day and I loved it.

The blacktop was slick and shiny, and the early afternoon lights lay in liquid trails in the thin film of water. The streets were empty and, freed from human observers, the oaks, sycamores and chestnut trees in the garden at the center of the square were all nodding sagely to each other, like they were deep in Entish dialogue.

I hadn't seen Gallin since she'd been assigned to work with me on the Helen Troy execution list in DC.[1] She had gone back to London, I had spent time convalescing, and we had kind of lost touch. Now I could see warm light in her living-room window and wondered if I should go and knock on the door. The moment's hesitation was resolved when the door opened and she stepped out with her collar turned up and an Irish, Donegal tweed cap on her head. She hunched her shoulders but didn't hurry. She trotted down the steps from her front lawn, glanced at me and came and opened the passenger door.

"Nice car!"

I smiled. "Hello stranger. Get in and you won't get wet."

She climbed in, slammed the door and removed her hat. Her hair was tied in a knot behind her head and now she untied it, retied it and tightened it as she spoke.

"It's been a long time. Months. What happened? Battery ran out on your phone?"

"Straight in, huh?" I smiled at her but she pretended to be busy with her hair. I shrugged and pulled away from the curb. At Notting Hill Gate I said, "I got the impression you were busy."

"I was," she said with something in her mouth. She took the something out and put it in her hair. "But I wasn't too busy to talk."

I shrugged again. It was a shrugging kind of conversation. "That wasn't the impression I got. You didn't call either."

"Well, ain't we like a couple of fifteen-year-old kids!"

"You know what Richard Bandler said—"

"He's back, Mr. Erudite Quotes. Bandler said a lot of things. That guy never shuts up. You hear his story about the guy who went to hospital with a ferret up his ass?" I looked at her. She said, "Sorry. What did he say, Alex?"

"Communication is always what the other person understands."

"Oh, that's very good. So, if to me 'kick you in the nuts' means 'have your babies' and I say to you, 'Alex, I want to have your babies,' but you understand, 'Alex, I want to kick you in the nuts,' that is what I have actually communicated?"

We had reached Marble Arch and I turned down Park Lane. The traffic there is like an intersection between the nine levels of hell. So I didn't answer until I'd turned left into Mount Street, left again into Park Street, cruised up among elegant, rain-washed Georgian buildings until as far as number thirty-seven (a grand, massive gray stone edifice five stories high, with great bay windows and elegant arches), and stopped the car. Then I looked at her.

"Yes, it is always wise to make sure we communicate what we want the other person to understand, rather than expect them to read our minds. Shall we go up?"

"Yeah," she said. "Let's go up."

The lobby was small, with a stone flagged floor and an old-fashioned elevator with a concertina door. I fitted a key I had been given by Nero to the panel where the buttons were, turned it, and the elevator carried us, squeaking and rattling, to a sixth floor the building appeared not to have. Gallin stared at me all the way. When the elevator had shuddered to a halt, she kept staring as she pulled back the concertina and we stepped out into a corridor of gray stone with a threadbare red carpet. At the end there was a large, oak door with a brass knob in the center.

I rang the bell and it was opened almost immediately by

a tall, angular woman in a knee-length gray skirt and a white blouse. She bent her knees slightly and smiled.

"Yes?" Her voice bordered on the shrill.

"I'm Alex Mason, this is Captain Aila Gallin."

She looked delighted, "Oh, *yes!*" she said. "*Do* come in. You don't mind if we just go through the steps." She closed the door and led us to what appeared to be a three-in-one printer on her desk, but turned out not to be. "Hand on there, look in here, don't move." We were scanned and processed and she gave a little clap. "There we are, all done! Super! Through that door over there, Sir John will see you straight away."

A door beside her desk opened and admitted us to another long, gray stone corridor. Halfway down on the left there was a door. A young man in a suit stepped out and grinned.

"Mr. Mason? Captain Gallin? How do you do? I am Nigel, Sir John's secretary. Please, this way, Sir John is expecting you." We followed him in to a small, cramped antechamber with a desk, a filing cabinet and a tray. "Can I bring you tea? Coffee?"

We declined and he opened yet another door into a very large, very comfortable office with a burgundy carpet, oak panels and glass-fronted bookcases. Sir John rose from a desk you could play billiards on, which he had positioned in a vast bay with tall Georgian windows behind him.

He was tall and had that peculiar, understated English elegance that you can only get by going to Winchester Boys' School and then Oxford.

"Captain Gallin, what a pleasure to meet you at last.

Your father and I are old friends. And Mr. Mason, Nero speaks very highly of you," his smile became humorous, "though I daresay he never lets on. Please, do sit."

We sat in red leather chairs and he sat across from us. He frowned and tapped his desk a few times with his pencil.

"Has Nero given you any idea what this is about?"

I shook my head. "No, not at all. All I know is that he has taken the unusual step of asking the Mossad to second Captain Gallin to us..."

"Yes, that was our request. I am in the UK branch of ODIN, you understand. What Nero is in the United States, I am here. When we had a look at the case, we thought it might be of interest to Israel."

I smiled pleasantly, feeling myself getting antsy. I was barely two hours off the plane and sorely in need of a couple of martinis and a primal steak. "What case?"

"Quite so, let me start at the beginning." He stood and walked to a dresser he had against one wall. There he poured three tumblers of whisky as he spoke.

"I am quite certain you have heard of Saul Epstein—"

I turned in my chair. "The TV show host? Investigative journalist. Specializes in big exposés."

"That's the chap. American, originally from Boston, though his parents were originally from Kent. Brilliant fellow, Harvard *and* Oxford, degree in history and doctoral thesis on the roots of social liberty in society. Bit of an Anglophile. Good read.

"Worked as a reporter on the *New York Times*, though he found their ethos uncongenial, then editor of the *Herald Tribune*, then moved to television production, anchor on nationally syndicated morning news and finally got his own show. What most people didn't realize was that he had settled in London some ten years ago and he used to shuttle back and forth to New York."

He carried over the glasses and set them on the desk. As he sat, I said, "Forgive me, Sir John, but—" I hesitated a moment, trying to find a diplomatic way of asking the question. "How does this affect ODIN?"

His eyebrows rose as he sipped. "Oh, well, he's dead."

"Oh—"

"Murdered."

"Oh, but I still don't see..."

"He was found by the janitor in his apartment on Kensington Church Street. ten PM, last Friday, 9th September."

I frowned and shrugged one shoulder. "It's a police matter."

His smile was thin, amiable and as friendly as a kick in the nuts. "If it were, Mr. Mason, I wouldn't have asked Nero to send his best man, and asked Gabriel Gallin to second us his best officer in London."

I returned him an equally thin smile. "I imagine you wouldn't, Sir John. What I meant to say was, what is it about this murder that makes it of interest to ODIN?"

"Allow me to tell you."

Gallin turned to me with a smile that was thinner than both of ours and said, "What Sir John is saying, Alex, is shut up and let him finish."

Sir John chuckled but didn't deny it.

"In recent years Saul had become increasingly...," he paused a moment, "I don't want to say obsessed, because that implies it was somehow irrational, and Saul was anything but irrational. But he had become extremely concerned with…"

Gallin sat forward, "Excuse me, Sir John." He looked at her with raised eyebrows. "You said, 'Saul'—you were on first-name terms?"

Again the thin smile. "We were close friends. Do you think that's relevant, Captain?"

"I don't know. And that's where I am going to file it."

"Splendid. So, he had become extremely concerned with what he saw as the overpopulation of the planet, nano-technology and genetic engineering. I asked him several times to clarify his concerns for me, but he refused. His precise words, the last time we spoke, were, 'When my research is finished, you'll be the first to read it.'"

Gallin spoke again, "What connects those three fields of research is that all three are concerned with very large numbers of people."

"Precisely."

"That and one other related point," I added. "Power. Power over not large, but immense sections of the population. Nano-technology applied to genetic engineering is a nightmare scenario from which we are separated by tissue paper."

"That is how Saul saw it. He said we could be looking at the fazing out of humanity over the next century or two. He said we had become redundant to ourselves."

"Visionaries." Gallin snorted. "In the past visionaries were dangerous because they started wars. Today visionaries have access to the technology to upgrade humanity, and terminate the race in the process. Yesterday's visionaries are today's messiahs and angels of death."

He nodded at his desk for a moment. "Some might accuse you of overstating the case, Captain Gallin, but I think you are right on the money. Saul would certainly have agreed with you. Today they are celebrities."

I said, "You think he was murdered because of his research." It wasn't a question. It was a conclusion.

"It seems likely. Saul was a popular man. He had very few enemies."

Gallin, quick as a viper, was in there. "Few..."

He shook his head sadly and took a sip of whisky. "Saul was not what you'd call handsome. But, from what I am told that is not necessarily a primary consideration with women." He glanced apologetically at Gallin. "Of course one has to be very careful with that kind of statement these days, one never knows what might be construed as offensive or misogynistic. However, in Saul's case, women seemed to be fascinated by him, despite his looks, and a physical condition which was, shall we say, marred by good living. He had been married three times. He was on reasonably good terms with his last wife, Julia, but he'd had a string of affairs. The last of these, Naomi Gordon, became very upset when she discovered that he had been having meetings with his ex-wife."

Gallin said, "Naomi Gordon? The model?"

"Yes, she's actually a highly intelligent woman, but venomously jealous. You know her, Mr. Mason?"

I shook my head. "Should I?"

Sir John cleared his throat. "Well, I mean, she is quite spectacular, really,"

Gallin cut him short. "Six-foot-one, black, but I mean *real* black, not Latina with a suntan, we are talking *ebony*. Built like a goddess, aquiline nose and almond eyes the size of small vases."

"Small vases?"

"Yeah, I couldn't think of anything almond shaped. All the way up legs. She was voted the most beautiful woman in the world by *Vogue* magazine or something." She turned a skeptical face to Sir John. "I didn't realize she had a brain though. Women that beautiful usually have brains like sparrow shit."

Sir John suppressed a laugh. "Yes, well, in her case she got a first in history from the LSE. Which," he then said "which" three times very quickly, "Which, which, which... *these* days does not perhaps mean as much as it might have done some years ago, but still. She is definitely an intelligent woman."

I said, "And she had it out for Saul Epstein because he had been seeing his ex-wife?"

"Yes. Julia, of course, is *extremely* intelligent. First class degree from Oxford in the classics—that was back in the 1980s, of course, when Oxford was still a good university. She then wrote her doctoral thesis on the subject of totalitarian societies, arguing that society pulls simultaneously, equally and irresistibly toward totalitarianism and anarchy, making a state of constant conflict inescapable. Saul found her fascinating. He often said that a good intellect was far more sexually arousing than a beautiful body. He was, he said, sapiosexual."

"Why'd they split up?"

"She left him. As well as sapiosexual, he was also plain

heterosexual and she found his philandering insulting, and in the end I think she found him a trifle childish."

Gallin scratched her head under her Irish tweed cap and made the face of skepticism. "You think Naomi Gordon was that crazy about him she'd kill him out of jealousy? I mean, she could have pretty much any man she wanted."

Sir John drew breath but I answered for him.

"That's not quite right, Gallin. In the first place, a lot of modern men feel intimidated by a woman like Naomi Gordon. Speaking purely sexually, a man needs a lot of vitality to satisfy a woman as intense as that. Most modern men, raised on a diet of fast food and vegan guilt, don't feel up to the job. If she is intelligent too, for every man she attracts, she is scaring off ten."

Gallin rolled her eyes. I ignored her and went on. "On the other hand, she doesn't need to be in love with Saul to feel rage. If her trophy man is having private meetings with his brilliant ex-wife, and that gets reported on social media, the humiliation for her would be huge. That would be enough to drive a narcissist to murder."

Sir John was nodding vigorously. "I agree with you one hundred and ten percent, on the...umm...second point. But equally I am certain that this was not what happened. Our concern—and let us pray that we are wrong—is that that he was assassinated because of the research he was doing, and that the research had to do with genetic engineering, over-population, and nano-technology."

"You have any leads? Any place we can start?"

He shook his head and stared at me for a moment. "That's why I asked Nero for you, and Gabriel for Captain Gallin. It is also one of the things that makes me quite certain it was an assassination. If Naomi had killed him, there would have been a frightful mess. But there is nothing, absolutely nothing, at the scene of the crime to indicate a crime has been committed, except the body. It takes a very good professional to do that."

I nodded a few times and Gallin nodded once and added, "It does."

# TWO

SIR JOHN HAD DROPPED A VERY THIN MANILA FILE on his desk and told us that was what there was of the police report. "We killed the police investigation as soon as we heard, but I shouldn't think they'd have got much further than they did anyway."

Inside, it contained the keys to Epstein's apartment, a couple of sheets of printed paper and a second envelope full of photographs.

After that he'd told us, "You may need to go beyond what is strictly legal, so we would be grateful if you would contact us as little as possible to ensure credible deniability. As you know, the Office of the Director of Information Networks requires the utmost secrecy."

"Your deniability is safe with us," I'd told him, and we left. On the way down in the 19th-century concertina elevator I had told Gallin, "You drive, I want to get carsick reading the report."

Now we were in the car weaving and battling through

traffic that did not benefit from the grid system because most of the winding, bending roads, streets, crescents, places, passages, ends, walks and mews were probably originally cattle tracks that dated back to the Neolithic age.

"Where are we going?" I asked as I tried to read.

"Well, Alex, I thought it might be a good idea to go and have a chat with Julia, his ex-wife. Ask me why. I promise you won't be encroaching on my privacy, my space or my work."

I took a deep breath and tried not to sigh.

"Why, Aila?"

"Well, for a start, she is apparently a highly intelligent woman, first class degree in the classics from Oxford—back in the 1980s when Oxford was still a good university—doctoral thesis in anthropology—plus, Saul found her so fascinating he couldn't keep his dirty little sapiosexual hands off her, despite the risk of being rejected." She gave me a look, like she had a meat grinder in her hands and was about to drop my testicles in it. "Jewish men are like that sometimes. We call them mensch. Or sometimes just, you know... men. A guy with balls who won't take no for an answer."

"Can we stay on task, Gallin."

I would have got more response from my late great-grandmother.

"A woman likes that sometimes. Shows a guy cares and is prepared to fight for what he wants. He calls: 'I need to see you, let's have dinner.' 'I can't. I'm busy.' 'Busy how? Make time.' 'I can't make time, Saul, I have a deadline!' 'Tell them you'll be late. I'm coming over. Wear something nice.'"

"Are you done?"

"Yes, Alex, my point is, she fascinated him, and being the

kind of *man* he was, there was none of this limp-wristed, 'I don't want to intrude, I respect your space' crap. So they must have been pretty close and *intimate*."

"So she might know something. OK, it's a good place to start."

"Yes, Alex."

We drove west along Kensington High Street, with the immensely green park on our right and huge, red busses all around us, till we came to Victoria Road. There we turned left among elegant Victorian mansions on the right and a grotesque monument to the Hive on the left. A short drive down we turned into Albert Place, a short, elegant street with more trees than houses. What houses there were had that solid elegance of the early decades of the 20$^{th}$ century. They were painted white or cream, with gray slate roofs, and were all partially hidden behind an abundance of foliage.

We pulled up outside a well-trimmed hedge and Gallin killed the engine. The windshield wipers gave two dying squeaks and stopped. Raindrops began to accumulate on the glass.

"Shall we go?"

She gave me a once-over with her eyes, nodded and got out.

By the time I'd got to the gate she had climbed the seven steps to the porch and was ringing on the brass bell beside the dark, glossy blue door. There was a rich smell of damp earth and autumn leaves on the air. The door opened as I came up beside her. There was a middle-aged woman holding the door and looking at us like we might be the next bad thing that was going to happen that day. She didn't say anything. She just clenched her fists and held them to her chest.

Gallin spoke first, "We are here to see Mrs. Epstein. Is she in?"

Her reply came in what the Brits call cut-glass English. It was also shrill and nasal. "She's indisposed. You'll have to go away and come back at another time!"

Gallin smiled and nodded. She had the same cut-glass English, only it wasn't shrill or nasal. "I'm sure she is. We are attached to Whitehall and we need to ask her some questions."

"No. I'm sorry. It's out of the question! Whitehall, you say?" She shook her head quickly. "No, sorry, makes no difference."

"The only problem is, if we go away and come back with a warrant, we'll have to bring police cars with sirens and it all gets very embarrassing."

The woman's jaw dropped. "That's outrageous!"

I nodded. "And noisy," I said. "It's very regrettable. Perhaps the simplest thing..." I shrugged and smiled.

She lifted her chin. "I shall go and speak to Mrs. Epstein. She may want to call her solicitor!"

"I hope not," I said with the nicest smile I had. "We really want to keep this discreet. The last thing the government wants is a media circus."

Her eyes went wide, she turned on her heel and marched away. She came back within a couple of minutes and spoke with cruel severity.

"You may come in! But *please*, be brief, and then leave!"

She led us past tasteful hunting prints to a spacious, elegant drawing room which was the more elegant for being slightly disordered and clearly enjoyed and lived it. There was a Georgian fireplace with a brass fireguard in front of it and a huge, pale gray calico sofa backing onto open French windows. Outside a lawn was turning slowly into a marsh and a metal barbeque was turning to rust. The only light was from the open windows, so half the room—the half with the armchairs in it—was in shadow.

Lying on the sofa was a woman in her sixties. Her hair had been a wild red, but was now streaked with occasional silver. She watched us with eyes that had learned to be ironic instead of bitter. You could read the intelligence in her face, and I could see why Saul had found her so attractive.

"A media circus? Seriously? Low, cheap blackmail." I was surprised to hear her accent was American. "I've let you in because I want Saul's killer caught, not because I am giving in to your threats. Who are you?"

Gallin showed her a fake ID she had apparently been supplied with, which said she was with Military Intelligence Section 5, and I showed her a plastic card that said I was with the Pentagon's Office of the Director of Intelligence which was true in an abstract sense; like Picasso's people with both eyes on the same side of their face.

She scrutinized both with interest and handed them back. "Neither of you is a cop. And you," she said, pointing at me, "you're from Washington. What's going on?"

I smiled again. I was doing a lot of smiling that morning, mainly at people who didn't appreciate it. "I *am* from Washington, Mrs. Epstein, and as you can probably tell this is a little complicated. I'd hate you to get a crick in your neck while we explain."

"Sit down, Alex Mason, and you'd better sit too,

Captain. I am extremely upset, so I hope you're not going to tax me. Why is Saul's death being investigated by spies instead of cops?"

Gallin snorted a small laugh. "That's pretty much what we hoped you would tell us."

Julia Epstein narrowed her eyes. "Run that by me again, sweet cheeks."

"Whitehall has asked us to look into your husband's—"

"Ex-husband—"

"Ex-husband's death because they believe there may be a political motive to the murder."

"As opposed to the more common motives of sex and money?"

Gallin nodded.

Julia shrugged and pulled down the corners of her mouth. "I guess the only person with any real motive to kill Saul for ordinary human reasons was me. He used to drive me mad. But every time I thought about shooting the bastard, I remembered how much I loved him."

Her lip curled in and she started to cry, without embarrassment or hysterics, looking down at a handkerchief she kept folding and unfolding. "I am really going to miss him. I miss him already."

"What about Naomi Gordon?" I asked.

"No." She shook her head. "You need strength of character to kill somebody. Either that or provocation beyond endurance. You know one, surefire way to tell whether someone has strength of character?"

"Tell me."

"If they are gifted with intelligence, and they make nothing of value out of their lives. Get a good degree! Write a book! Discover something! Help people! Make your life valuable somehow! But get rich by showing the world what a great body you've got?" She leaned forward, turning from me to Gallin as she spoke. "*Why the hell isn't that girl frustrated out of her mind? I'll tell you.*" She sank back into the sofa again. "Because she is a narcissist, with no ambition, and no strength of character. She would not kill Saul. She *could* not kill Saul. The best she could do in the way of punishing him would be to have herself photographed with as many beautiful, sexually ambiguous men as possible, with her mouth wide open in a mindless grin, post them on her social media pages or whatever the hell they are, and hope that he'd feel jealous. That's it. Virtual revenge through virtual pain."

Gallin stepped in and pulled us back on track.

"We understand you had a pretty tight friendship, and Mr. Epstein confided in you."

"That's true up to a point. I was probably the only person in the world Saul actually loved. He was a selfish, domineering bastard with no time for weak people. At the same time, he was noble. He was on a crusade to expose the sons of bitches who exploit, denigrate and abuse humanity. It sounds contradictory, but he used to say he was with Snoopy. He loved mankind, it was people he couldn't stand. So, if he shared any details of his research or investigation with anyone, it would be me." She shook her head. "But he hardly ever mentioned any details about his investigations."

Gallin leaned forward. Her eyes were intense. "I don't want to pressure you, Mrs. Epstein, but you may be the only person who has any clue at all as to who murdered Saul, and why. Is there anything, however trivial, you can think of that might help us to know what he was working on? Any passing comments, names he mentioned, people he'd been in touch with..."

"Back in the day he was friends with William Rees-Mogg. Rees-Mogg was an intellectual, a lateral thinker, politically involved and totally radical, a fascinating guy. He talked to Saul about nano-technology and how it was going to change society. That made an impact on Saul and he became more and more obsessed with it as the technology advanced. And in the last two or three years, that was all he would talk about, nano-technology, genetic engineering *using* nano-technology, and what he called 'the darkness' that was enveloping the planet. The new Dark Age."

Gallin frowned. "What did he mean by that?"

"According to Saul, humanity is a plague. Trouble is, we are also at the top of the food chain. And according to him that meant that we would be driven, by nature itself, to destroy ourselves. The more we swarmed over the globe, the more self-destructive our behavior would become. And he particularly saw this in the elite. Those with absolute temporal power. The billionaire club—those who count their billions in tens and hundreds. He was increasingly convinced that they had an agenda to cull humanity—"

"Excuse me?" It was Gallin, frowning.

"You heard me right, honey—*cull*. That is the word he used. There are too many of us, and what do you do with a species when there are too many of them? You cull them."

"Forgive my saying so, Mrs. Epstein, but it sounds like the kind of science fiction conspiracy theory you find on the internet."

She laughed. "Oh, I forgive you and I agree with you. And that was what I told Saul, only not so nicely. And you know what he said? He looked at me and he said, 'Science fiction, Julia? Like Asimov and *Star Trek*? We left science fiction behind a long time ago.' He said, 'The technology to do what I am talking about already exists. All that is missing is the political will to do it.' And then he asked me, 'Or is it?'" She spread her hands, washing them of any involvement in Saul's crazy ideas. "Anyway, you asked me what he was working on. That's as much as I know about what he was working on."

I asked, "Did he give you any names of corporations or people?"

"Not that I can recall." She frowned, like she was having trouble understanding something. "I am very tired, and I'd like to be alone with my thoughts now. If I think of anything, I'll let you know."

I nodded. "Of course. I am really very sorry." I stood and took out my card. As I set it on the table beside her I said, "Just before we go, who were his close friends, his intimate circle?"

Her face became depressed. She gave her head a helpless little shake. "Me. People he had close contact with? Well, his producer, obviously, that's Pamela, Pamela Peach-Plum, and that playboy philanderer..." She thought for a moment. "... His lawyer, Nick, Nick Barnes. They were the only people he had close contact with. And Naomi, of course, but that was just sex. He had no respect for her as a person."

When we stepped outside, the rain had eased to a slight drizzle, but the eaves, guttering and upper floor windowsills were dripping in a wet, broken rhythm. Occasional cars passed nearby with a wet sigh. Everything was wet.

I descended the steps to the sidewalk with Gallin behind

me. I went to the passenger side and leaned on the roof, making my sleeves wet. She opened the driver's door and stopped, looking at me.

"What?"

I screwed up my face in thought. "Epstein's apartment. Then we need a pub with a fire and meat pies."

She nodded. "Sure." She climbed in and I got in next to her. "His apartment is just up the road, in Church Street."

We pulled away and turned up toward the High Street. She drove in silence. Finally I said, "We need to clear the air, Gallin. Or this is going to interfere with our work."

She held up two fingers in the V sign. "One, I have worked very efficiently many times with people I really did not like, in sullen silence, and we got the job done very efficiently. You don't need to get on well with someone to work well with them. Two, is that your main reason for wanting to clear the air? To make sure it does not prejudice the job?"

I rolled my eyes and asked the gods to give me patience.

"Yes, of course it is possible. No, that is not my main reason. Gallin, this is getting out of hand. We need to stop."

"Yup, and the longer you avoid it, the worse it's going to get. Alex, I am this far," she held up her thumb and forefinger and they were practically touching, "*this far*, from telling you to go to hell." I drew breath but she cut me short. "Tell me one more time that it is affecting our work and I *will* tell you to go to hell."

"OK, that was a poor choice of words—"

"And don't even *dream*," she said as we turned into Church Street, "of proving your feminist credentials to me by showing how sensitive you are and revealing your feminine side."

I drew breath again but she cut me short again. "You don't want to stay in touch? That's fine. You don't need to explain yourself to me. We just do the job and get it done. You go back to DC, I stay home in London. Sorted."

"OK, Gallin, you made your point! Now shut up and let me talk, will you?"

She slammed on the brakes and skidded to a halt by the curb. A car honked behind us and then passed with an angry glare. I stared at Gallin and she jerked her chin at my door. "Get out."

"*What?*"

"Get out! We're here. This is his apartment block."

She climbed out and made her way toward the building. I sat a moment swearing softly under my breath, then got out and went after her.

# THREE

We stood at the open door looking across a broad expanse of parquet floor strewn here and there with Persian rugs that had that exquisitely imperfect genuine look. The nearest one was about twelve feet away and the nearest edge was stained a deep rust color. The floor bordering the rug was also stained with rusty, coagulated blood which had pooled and oozed out to the sides before drying and caking.

Gallin had the manila file open in her hands and was reading it. I said:

"Thumbprint on the doorbell?"

"There isn't. it's the first thing SOCO did."

"SOCO?"

"Scene of Crime Officers. The forensic team."

"What was he, about six foot?"

"Six one."

"So he is lying with his head here," I moved into the

room, where the carpet was stained, "on the edge of the carpet, on his back, with his feet toward the door."

She was looking at the photograph, glanced at me and nodded, biting her lip. I went on, "So this is curious..."

She said, "If you're pointing a gun at an unarmed person, threatening to shoot them, they instinctively hold their hands up to try and ward off the shot. A shot to the head like that, death is instantaneous. So he went down exactly like he was standing."

I was nodding. "Hands down by his side, in a natural, standing position."

"Which you'd expect if he had just opened the door. But he is, what, three or four strides from the door?"

"Yeah," I agreed. "But he is not walking away, because he is *facing* the door."

"So the killer rings at the bell, he comes and opens the door, 'Oh, it's you,' and walks away talking over his shoulder, 'Come on in, grab a beer.' But the guy closes the door and says, 'Hey, Saul, look at this.' Saul turns and the killer shoots him in the head."

"Yeah, OK, I buy that. Questions: One, where was he when the doorbell rang? Two, same question put another way, where was he going back to? He wasn't shaking hands and saying, 'Oh, hi. Come on in, let me take your coat.' No, he was interrupted and he was returning to something he wanted to get back to quickly."

She walked past me and made her way to the kitchen. I followed her and found the kitchen pristine. She turned to face me. "He wasn't cooking. The TV was not turned on. There were no books or magazines open on the lamp tables. That leaves just one thing."

"His study."

Gallin went inside and I leaned on the doorjamb. She made a face like mental constipation and I sighed deeply and scratched my head. There was nothing there. A single narrow French window open onto a small wrought-iron balcony. There were bookcases jammed with books and a desk with nothing on it. She turned to face me and rested my ass on the desk. I said:

"What does the police report say?"

"Nothing. It makes no mention."

"Time of death? Last seen…?"

"He was found Friday, September 9th at ten PM. Last time he was seen alive, as far as the cops were able to ascertain, was Thursday the 8th, the day before, about 9 PM. He went to visit Naomi. He may have been seen after that, but the cops only had the case about twenty-four hours."

"So no precise time of death."

She shrugged. "Some time between nine PM Thursday and ten PM Friday. Twenty-five hours. We can trim that a little, but not much."

"And nothing from forensics."

"Squat. There was no casing, so he may have used a revolver. A .45 revolver makes a lot of noise. But these apartments have thick old walls. The prints in the apartment are his, Naomi's, the janitor's and a couple of others that got no hits on Five Eyes' databases or ours."

She was quiet for a moment, then snorted suddenly. "So here's what we have: The killer was known to Saul, who admitted him voluntarily and invited him in as he hurried to get back to—absolutely nothing at all—then stopped after three strides to turn around and get shot—one single, clean shot right through the head."

"What we have is a very peculiar situation. At its most basic, Saul was working on his research, the doorbell rang and he went to open it. Now we have two options, the killer was disguised as a pizza delivery kid and Saul was hurrying to get his wallet—"

She shook her head. "His billfold was in his pocket."

"Or he knew his killer well enough to invite him in, in a very casual way while he hurried back to his work. As we have already said, the friend called to him, asked him to hold up or something, and when he turned around he shot him. Then he went to the study and recovered the material Saul was working on."

"Right now that is about the only explanation that makes sense."

"But it raises the most extraordinary requirement, that one of Saul's closest friends—you know, the kind of friend who you tell, 'Come on in, grab a beer, turn on the game, I'm just finishing up!'—that friend, is a highly trained professional killer."

She gave a small, humorless laugh and gazed out at Church Street through the narrow French windows. "Doesn't seem very likely, does it?"

"Not really, but what else have we got?"

She hunkered down and went through the desk drawers, then scoured the rest of the office, looking in cupboards, folders, plastic bags full of papers and glass jars on the desk. She even examined the upholstery on his chair. Finally she sat on the floor and looked up at me.

"His computer is gone, his external hard drives and USB

drives are gone. Any notes he had are gone. The guy just came in, collected up Saul's work and left with it. Point to note." She raised a finger and wagged it at me. "Either the killer didn't mind wiping out an entire cocktail party if he had to, or he knew that Saul was alone."

"Yeah, or he knew Saul well enough that if there was some kind of social gathering, he'd be welcomed in."

She nodded. "The conclusion is the same—the point that emerges over and over from all this is that the killer is part of Saul's intimate circle."

I said, "Yeah," and then, embarrassingly, we both spoke at the same time, "Only Saul has no intimate circle."

A voice behind me made me start and turn. It was a pleasant, modulated voice that sounded educated, but I still found myself reaching for my weapon, though all it said was, "Hello...?"

I walked toward it. "Who's there?"

"Simon," it replied, "the maintenance man."

Simon the maintenance man came into view in the corridor from the drawing room. He was wearing blue overalls and had a pencil behind his ear, but I was surprised to see he was in his early twenties and had the bearing and demeanor of what the Brits call a public school boy, by which they mean the product of one of the most expensive schools on the planet. He studied me a moment, then studied Gallin a few feet behind me in the study doorway.

"Who are you?" he said, with some spirit.

I pointed to Gallin. "That is Captain Aila Gallin, she works for Section Five of Military Intelligence. My name is—"

"Have you got some ID?" He was talking to Gallin. She

arched an eyebrow at him. "I am not required to show you any ID, Simon."

"No, but you will be required to show it to the police, and they'll be here in about ten minutes after I phone them. I am responsible for the care and maintenance of these apartments, and I would like to know who you are and what you are doing here. I have been very civil so far, and I do not think my request to see documentation is unreasonable. I could, if you prefer, call my uncle at Milbank."

I smiled at Gallin. "Isn't that where your headquarters are located, Gallin, at Milbank? Just show Simon your ID."

She showed him her fake ID card and he inspected it like he knew what he was looking for. He handed it back and said, "It's authentic."

"I know."

He turned to me. "Who are you?"

"Alex Mason, I work for the Pentagon, the Office of the Director of Intelligence. You haven't got another uncle in Arlington, have you?"

I gave him my card and he scrutinized it and muttered offhand, "No, of course not." He handed it back. "I assume you're here about Mr. Epstein's death, but what are you doing? Who let you in? What authority have you got?"

Gallin answered him. "OK, Simon, I want you to listen very carefully to what I am going to tell you. You are very observant and you will have noticed that the police have stopped investigating. In such a high-profile case that is unusual to say the least. Now, that has happened because they have handed over the case to us, and we are cooperating with the Americans. Saul was an American, and some of his investigative journalism used to go very deep into some pretty sensitive territory. And we think that might be what got him killed. So we now have jurisdiction over this crime scene. If you want to go check with the police or your uncle, be my guest. But as you're here and you have seen our ID, it would be a damn sight more helpful if you stayed and helped us."

"How? Will you pay me? I don't live on air, you know?"

I said, "You found the body, right?"

He nodded. "Sometimes Mr. Epstein had lady friends who would stay. Sometimes they would just stay the night. Sometimes they would stay for two or three days. He couldn't tolerate them much more than that."

I laughed. "He couldn't tolerate them?"

"That's what he told me. After sixty hours they stopped pleasing him and started getting on his nerves."

"He told you that?"

"Yes. He used to talk to me a lot. He would go for long periods where no women would visit him. That was usually when he was working on a project and needed to avoid distraction. During those times he would call me sometimes and send me to buy whisky, or cigarettes, and when I brought them he would tell me to sit down and we would talk."

I crossed my arms and leaned against the wall. "Son of a gun!"

His eyes searched my face. "Is that surprising, Mr. Mason?"

It was one of three times I have felt acutely embarrassed in my entire life. "No," I said, "not at all. That's not what I..."

"I am extremely dyslexic, Mr. Mason, and I am also

highly dyspraxic. That doesn't mean I can't read and I'm clumsy. It simply means I process information differently, and crowds stress me and make me feel inadequate and I make mistakes. I also suffer from Asperger's, which is on the autistic spectrum, and makes it very difficult for me to deal with people. So I chose to work here, where I am in control of my space and the people I deal with—most of the time.

"However, my father is Sir Bob Hamilton, he's in the diplomatic corps, and we frequently travel to Washington. My mother is a professor of anthropology at the University of London and lectures regularly at Arizona State University. Though they don't give me any money. And when I graduated from Westminster Boys' School I was offered a place at Oxford to read the classics. Which I declined. Because, Mr. Mason, I don't like people."

"Understood. My apologies. But you liked Saul."

He looked at the floor and nodded. "Yes."

Gallin said gently, "So Saul asked you to go get something for him that day?"

"No, the day before. He had given me money and asked me to go and get him some cigars. But I had had other things to do. I had to visit Mummy and Daddy, and have dinner with them. Then they convinced me to stay over, and in the end it wasn't until ten PM in the evening of Friday the 9<sup>th</sup> that I was finally able to bring him his cigars. And that was when I found him."

"What did you do?" I asked him.

He eyed me a moment. "I didn't touch the body. It was clear he was dead. His skin was a terrible gray color. His eyes were open and he had a black, slightly crusted hole in his forehead. My guess was a .45, which makes a slightly larger hole than a 9mm. I know that from hunting in Arizona. So it was very obvious that he was dead, and had been for a while."

"So what *did* you do?"

His gaze became abstracted. "There were just a couple of lamps on in the drawing room. The rest of the apartment was dark, except for his study..." His gaze rose to the study behind Gallin. "Down there. There I could see light and I wondered if somebody had broken in to steal his work. It was unlikely they would still be here, because he had been dead for a long time, but I went down to have a look."

Gallin said, "That was brave."

"Not really, Captain. I am skilled in self-defense, and I do lots of courses in the United States on survival and combat techniques. It's my hobby. But when I got to the study, obviously there was nobody there."

"Wait." I raised a hand. "There was no*body* there. But what *was* there? On the desk. Can you remember?"

"Yes, I have a very good memory. There was nothing there. It was as you have just seen it now. Normally he would have had his long notepad by his left hand, with a black uni-ball fine pen, the keyboard in front of him, the mouse on his right and the big screen also in front of him. But all that was gone."

"OK, so you say you had seen him a couple of days before that. Did you happen to go into his office?"

"Yes, he was very happy. He said he had finished his work and now he was going to devote his time to writing his auto-biography. He joked that he might even marry Naomi Gordon. I told him not to."

"What was on the desk?"

"What I just described to you."

"But what about the work he said he'd finished. That must have been bundled up on the desk somewhere, right?"

He pushed past me and Gallin and walked to the study. He stood there a long time staring at the desk. "No," he said at last. "It had been there for months. It had been all over the place. Piles of papers, reference books, USB drives, even old DVDs. But all of that was gone. As he'd said. He'd finished."

Gallin said, "Think really hard, Simon. Where would he have put it? Where would he have kept it?"

"I don't need to think very hard. I have no idea. He would not confide a thing like that to me. I assume his producer or his solicitor would have it." He looked from Gallin to me and back again. "I think I would like to leave now. I will have to inform his ex-wife, or his executor, that you were here."

"Sure, that's no problem at all, Simon. Thank you, you have been very helpful."

I gave him ten pounds. He looked unhappy about leaving us there, but left. I followed him to the door and closed it behind him. Then turned to face Gallin. She was watching me from across the room. She said, "Let's just contemplate a parallel angle. Humor me." She stood and leaned on the back of the sofa. "I think Mrs. Epstein has enough love, betrayal and anger in her to drive her to kill, if the right provocation were there..."

"What provocation? They're already divorced."

"But she thinks he's coming back to her, they're having intimate conversations, enough to make Naomi mad, right?" She wagged a finger at me again. "And I think she's right.

Naomi is vain, but she's no killer. Julia, on the other hand, has enough passion and enough strength of character to kill."

"That is one hell of an assertion, Gallin."

"Yeah, well, I have known a lot of killers and a lot of people who could not kill. Hear me out. Saul is getting on and starts gravitating back to her because she is the only woman who has ever really touched him emotionally. The only woman who has ever satisfied his sapiosexual lust. She starts to think that maybe he wants a reconciliation, and they will be together in their final years. But Saul is that typical, self-involved asshole who is all about what he needs and never thinks about what the *other* person might need. But now, in their last meeting, he does something, says something, he *tells* her something, that really hurts her."

"Like what?"

She nodded. "Like what Simon has just told us. Naomi has been giving him a hard time, demanding commitment. So he tells her he is thinking of marrying her. Remember, this guy is vain too. He loves his status. He is the macho hell-raiser who fearlessly exposes the bad guys, and gets the most beautiful, exotic women, half his age. He has Julia there to use her, to console him when he needs somebody to understand his complex, brilliant mind. But the reward goes to Naomi for being the most beautiful woman in the world."

I sighed at how feasible it was. "Hell hath no fury."

"Hell hath no fury like a woman scorned."

"It's depressingly possible. But if she killed him out of rage, why was she so cool about it? Why the single shot? Why didn't she empty the magazine into him? *And a .45?*

And above all, why did she remove his computer and his papers?"

I watched her eyes narrow and flit over my face. She gave a little shrug. "People experience rage in different ways. In some people it's a loss of control. In others it becomes extreme control. As to the computer, what she took was his autobiography. That manuscript is worth a fortune, even unfinished. She didn't want anybody else to get their hands on that."

I grunted.

She said, "I want to know a lot more about Julia Epstein." She pulled out her cell and walked away toward the study. She spoke quietly.

"Yeah, hi. Julia Epstein...uh-huh, have we got a file on her? Have a look, will you. I want everything we have on her... Yeah, thanks. You too."

I was leaning against the doorjamb when she came back in, putting her phone back in her pocket.

"You had to walk away for that?"

She didn't answer and I pulled out my own cell, feeling suddenly angry. I confirmed my identity and as Lovelock came on the line I went and stood right next to Gallin, looking down into her face. "Hey, Lovelock, listen, Saul Epstein was married to a woman in London, an American, her name is Julia. Can you get the nerds to get together everything we have on her? From the day she was born till today... You're a doll. Thanks."

I hung up. Her expression was pugnacious. I said, "You want to grab a meat pie and a beer, or do you want to go and eat alone and we meet up later?"

"What do *you* want? You want me to leave you alone?"

"I want you to stop behaving like a fifteen-year-old and allow me to clear the air without causing a traffic accident."

"We'll go to the Churchill. It's a short walk."

"Fine."

# FOUR

WE WENT DOWN IN THE ELEVATOR IN SILENCE AND stepped out into the wet street. Everyone seemed to be walking at a thirty to forty-five-degree angle, collars up, umbrellas up, legs stiffly striding. Gallin pulled up her collar and stuffed her hands in her pockets. I fell into step beside her. I heard her sniff and saw that she had small drops of water accumulating on her cheeks and on her nose.

"Look, I am not a mensch..."

"You are."

"*What?*"

"You are. That's part of the problem."

For a moment my brain hurt. I said, "Look, don't talk, OK? Just try not to talk for a bit." She shrugged and I went on—almost. "You..." I said and wiped rain from my face. "There was that...uh...your last night..." I glanced at her to see if she was going to help me out. Her face said she wasn't. I sighed. "I thought... But then you fell asleep. And I..."

"I'd had half a bottle of Irish whiskey on top of half a bottle of red wine and a couple of beers."

"Yeah, me too."

"You're six foot two and weigh over two hundred pounds. I'm five foot six in heels and I weigh as much as one of your legs."

"Stop arguing with me. I'm not discussing this. I'm telling you what happened. I thought you regretted..."

I took a deep breath and we pushed into the warmth of the Churchill. It was almost empty. We leaned on the bar and I told the barman, "Two steak and kidney pies and two pints of your best bitter."

He pulled the pints and we carried them to a table by the window. It was made up of leaded diamond shapes and through them you could see the big, wet red buses warping slowly down the road. Gallin said, "You can order two steak and kidney pies and two pints of beer, but you can't finish a single sentence when you talk to me."

I took another deep breath. "There was all the stuff I said while I couldn't speak—[1]"

"Boy, communication is the big thing with you, huh?"

"Stop it. You heard some of what I said." She nodded. "And we both got..."

"Say it!"

"Fond!"

"Jesus, Mary and sweet Joanna!"

"And I thought you had decided that... that you regretted... Dammit! That you thought it would be a mistake to... that you *didn't want to...*"

"Have sex?"

"Yes!"

"*Make love?*"

"*Yes!* So you fell asleep instead. And once you had gone, you went silent—"

"Correction. *You* went silent."

"I am telling you what *I* thought. Not what you thought. And to me it seemed you were trying to cool things off."

"Like I have ever done that. So *would* it have been a mistake?"

"For me or for you?"

"For you."

"No!"

Her cheeks flushed. "We can't have this conversation now."

"*What?*"

"It's going to get in the way of the job." She pulled off half her pint, belched softly and said, "There's the food."

I watched her go to the bar, collect the food and order two more pints. When she got back she set the plates down and the basket of cutlery and grinned at me. "I got the food, now you go get the beers."

I collected them from the bar and as I sat, still wondering what had just happened, she said, "That's what happened to Julia and Saul."

"What...?" It wasn't so much a "what happened to Julia and Saul?" as just a generalized, universal, *What?*

"They stopped communicating." She cut into her pie and let the meaty, aromatic steam waft out. "It's a recurrent theme with Saul. He is this great communicator. He communicates to millions of people and people go out of their way to watch him and listen to him because he is such a great communicator." She picked up a fry from her basket and bit it. "Not just easy to listen to, but packed with accurate, well-researched information. Not a good communicator, a *great* communicator. And yet..." She selected the largest of her fries, and waved it at me. "Among his friends and family, he was a crap communicator. He was all about himself and his secrets. Is that irony?"

"I guess it might be."

"Communication," she said again and cut a chunk of her pie. "Communication."

"Gallin," I said, screwing up my face, "are you aware of everything you've just done?"

She returned my frown with her fork still in her mouth and nodded. "Mm-hmm."

"Oh—"

"Get a grip, Mason. This is going to be a very complex case. Nothing is what it seems and everything will be bewildering."

I turned my attention to my steak and kidney pie, telling myself she had at least stopped calling me Alex. I turned my attention to the steaming hot pie and the deep, rich beer.

———

THERE IS a single road that runs from the west coast of Wales for over five hundred miles all the way through West London and the heart of the city. It then goes on out toward the east coast where it peters out and dies in Essex. It has lots of names: the A40, the M40, Ealing Broadway, Acton High Street and Oxford Street are but a few of them.

We were now, after a very fortifying luncheon, on the

section of that road where Acton High Street becomes Ealing Broadway. We were inching along at about three miles an hour, being steadily overtaken by furiously striding, wet frowning people dressed in plastic, while our windshield wipers ticked away the pointless seconds of our damp existence.

I had decided I had zero interest in Naomi Gordon. A decision which had caused Gallin to arch her eyebrows and sigh. I had ignored her and decided further that our priorities should be Saul's producer, Pamela Peach-Plum, and the philandering Nick Barnes, his lawyer.

"Don't discount the possibility, Mason, that this is an act of jealousy that looks like a conspiracy because of the setting, and the people involved. If the president's jealous lover sticks a pair of scissors in his heart, it does not mean the Chinese paid an assassin tailor to do it."

I thought about arguing the point, but let it slide instead. We finally arrived at Ealing and turned into the Common, where we soon came to a large Victorian house with a discreet sign outside that said it was the White Rabbit Studios. I killed the engine and climbed out. Late afternoon was inching toward dusk. There was a breeze that had turned cold, and the sky that sagged over the huge chestnut trees was a deep, gunmetal gray.

I shuddered and the wind threw a couple of wet, bronze leaves at my ankles. I kicked them off and we crossed the sidewalk to push through the small iron gate. There was a paved path across a sodden lawn strewn with more russet leaves. Seven redbrick steps led to an oxblood door, where Gallin rang the bell.

The door was opened by a thin, pale girl with short, very

black hair. She seemed to be wearing her obese great-grandfather's dungarees and plastic flip-flops. Her feet were pink and I felt cold for them.

She said, "Hi!" like she wasn't sure if she should know who we were or not.

I said, "We're here to see Pamela Peach-Plum." Which wasn't exactly a lie. That was the reason we were there. It just happened to suggest we had an appointment, which we hadn't, because she wouldn't answer her phone.

"Oh," said the girl, taken off balance. She opened her hands and glanced around, as though seeking help. I came to her aid with a smile. "Is she not back yet?"

The look she flashed me was one of gratitude and hope. "Oh!" she said again. "Do you know where she is?"

I looked at Gallin. "I mean, I don't know where she went after lunch... I just assumed she'd be here. Did she say anything to you?"

Again, none of it was a lie. Gallin thought about it, shook her head and said, "No, I just assumed, like you..."

I glanced at my watch. "I wouldn't have thought she'd be long. Do you mind if we wait in her office?"

"No! Sure, of course, um..."

We followed her through a large busy entrance hall where people were working hard at looking creative. We followed her up a flight of stairs and wound up in a disorganized office overlooking the Common.

"Tea?" She said it with a big smile, like there at least she was on safe ground.

"No, thanks, we'll be just fine."

She showed me a lot of teeth and said, "Just shout if you need anything. I'm sure she won't be long."

She left and I stood leaning on the doorframe, blocking the view, while Gallin moved with speed around the office looking for anything with Epstein's name on it. After ten minutes she'd had no joy, but just as we were about to give up, a middle-aged guy in a striped shirt and horn-rimmed glasses stuck his head in the door and eyed us a moment.

"Are you looking for Pamela?"

"Yup." I nodded.

"Have you seen her today?"

Gallin said, "We were supposed to."

"But you didn't?"

"No, why?"

He gave a small, uncertain sigh. "She hasn't shown up today, she hasn't called in, she's not at home and she isn't answering her phone. If you know anything..." He gave his head a quick shake. "I mean, I don't know if I should call the police..."

I reached for my wallet. "This is Captain Aila Gallin. She is with Section Five." She showed him her fake ID and I showed him my real one. "And I am seconded from the Pentagon. We need to talk to Ms. Peach-Plum urgently. Can you please give us her address?"

"Well, I don't know if..."

"We can get a warrant, but that delay could cost her her life. I'm pretty sure you wouldn't want to be responsible for that."

"Oh," he said, his face showing sudden realization. "You're here about Saul."

"What do you know about that?"

"Nothing, absolutely nothing at all. I'll get you her address."

He left and came back ten minutes later with a card. He handed it to me and said, "Tell her to call in if you see her, will you?"

Gallin asked him, "Do you work together? On the same projects?"

He sighed heavily this time and looked away. "Look, we all chip in a bit, but I really..."

"This is a murder investigation, Mr...."

"Noon, Sean Noon."

"And concealing evidence is an offence."

"I am not concealing evidence! I just don't *know* anything."

"Did she discuss Epstein's investigation with you?"

"Never."

"If I close down your studio and work through your staff one by one, none of them is going to recall you discussing that project with Pamela?"

He rubbed his face and pushed past us into her office where he half sat on the desk.

"I know *practically* nothing," he said with emphasis. "She was very excited about it. She was talking about ICFJ awards, Pulitzer..." He waved a vague hand. "She was really excited, and so was he. She even said it would be bigger than Watergate, which is patently ridiculous. She was not a woman given to hyperbole, he even less so, but *he* was the one who knew everything, and he's dead. She just went by what he told her."

Gallin pressed him. "If they went that far, they must have given you some idea what it was about."

His face turned queasy. "Quite honestly, it sounded like science fiction. Nobody would take it seriously. They were ranting about nano-technology, genetic engineering... Frankly I thought they'd both taken leave of their senses."

I sucked air through my teeth, staring at the rain out the window. "Can you remember any other details, names, corporations..."

"Yes, but again I didn't believe it was real. It was too ridiculous. They were talking about some stupid name— the..." He frowned, thinking. "The Foundation for Computer and Cybernetic Information Technology."

Gallin rolled her eyes. "Cute."

"Yes, their tagline is apparently, Just Do It."

I smiled. "FUCCIT Just Do It?"

"Yes, I have to say I have never heard of them."

"So what was the story?" I asked. "This foundation was engaged in nano-technology and genetic engineering?"

"Probably, but I honestly wasn't paying attention because I thought it was all a load of nonsense." He gave a small shrug and added quietly, "Then Saul showed up dead. But honestly, knowing Saul, it was probably some jealous husband, or one of his many women!"

"Maybe so. Where would she have kept it?"

"What?"

I arched my eyebrows high. "The work, the documentary, the manuscript, the research..."

He made like a goldfish for a while, goggling at me and opening and closing his mouth. Finally he said, "Oh, oh, um, Saul. Saul would have held on to that. I'm sure. Definitely, I think. Almost certainly, for sure."

I studied him a moment, then gave him my card. "We're going to see if we can find Pamela at home. If you hear from her in the meantime, or she shows up, tell her it is imperative she contacts us right away. She could be at risk."

He looked doubtfully at the card. "What about the rest of us?"

OUTSIDE IT HAD STOPPED RAINING. The air was fresh and smelled strongly of wet grass. On the blacktop, the cold evening breeze made tiny waves in the puddles. Gallin went round to the passenger side, hesitated before opening the door and leaned her forearms on the wet roof.

"He finishes his research. He is ready to start shooting, and they both decide this documentary is going to make him a byword in international, investigative journalism. This is going to be Watergate on steroids."

I nodded, with my hands in my pockets, making little splashes in the puddles with the toes of my shoes. She went on.

"Then, suddenly, in rapid succession, five things happen: one," she raised a finger, "he starts getting close with Julia again; two, Naomi finds out and gets mad; three, he gets executed; four, all his research disappears; and, five, so does his producer—all within a matter of a few days. There is no way these events are not connected."

I grimaced at the wet blacktop. "I agree, but I'm damned if I can see how at the moment."

"OK. How does this work? Let's go through it by stages. He finishes his research and shows it to Pamela. They both agree it's dynamite. He's looking at the Pulitzer, a best-selling book, the works. So the first thing they are going to do is make sure the material is put somewhere safe."

I looked at her under my eyebrows for a moment as I continued to tap puddles and make nano-tsunamis. "OK, that's good. So it's either up in her office, where we just were, or it's at her house, or..."

"Or it's with Nick Barnes."

I stopped making waves and nodded a few times. "Yup." I opened the driver's door, but Gallin kept talking, leaning on the roof of the car. Apparently she wasn't cold or damp.

"He's reached an age where he feels he needs more than passing affairs, or a harem of adoring women—he needs a woman who is also a companion, who is strong enough and intelligent enough to share his life. Now he feels he has nailed his crowning achievement, or is about to, and so he dumps Naomi and starts making eyes at Julia—that is the extent to which they enter into this."

You said, not half an hour ago—"

"Forget that. I changed my mind." She held my eye a moment. "But he has stepped on the toes of some powerful, secretive people in the military-industrial complex during his investigation, and they have taken him out. Sir John's hunch was right on the money."

"OK, so, Pamela Peach-Plum's house, Nick Barnes and some research into FUCCIT. And somewhere along the line bed. I still need to check in to my hotel."

I climbed behind the wheel and she got in beside me, dialing on her phone. As I turned around and headed back toward the Broadway, she said, "Mr. Nick Barnes, please. Captain Aila Gallin."

She waited, watching the darkening park slip by, then sat forward slightly. "Mr. Nick Barnes? My name is Captain Aila Gallin, I am attached to Section Five of Military Intelligence. It is imperative we speak to you as soon as possible regarding Saul Epstein's murder."

She put it on speaker and placed it on the dash.

"I'm sorry, did you say Military Intelligence?"

"Section Five, sir—MI5."

"What on Earth has Saul's death got to do with MI5?"

"Well, sir, that is something I would rather not discuss on a mobile phone. Where and when is it convenient for you to meet with us?"

"Well, it's a bit late now. You'd better come to my office tomorrow morning. I'll be there at eight. But please be punctual. I have a heck of a day and I'll be traveling later."

He gave her the address and hung up.

The traffic had eased and we cruised through the failing light as the headlamps and the streetlamps started to come on. The rain couldn't make up its mind. It was like it was bored with raining, but there was still too much water in the clouds. So there'd be an occasional squall, which would stop suddenly and leave your wipers squeaking on a dry windshield.

Pamela Peach-Plum lived in a big, white Victorian house in Arundel Gardens, in Notting Hill. She had four floors plus an attic and a basement, a stoop and a big bow window. That one, and all the others, were dark. Gallin had called her number several times on the way, but still got no reply.

I reached in my pocket and pulled out my Swiss Army knife. Gallin shouldered me gently out of the way. "You still using the tricks you learned on the mean streets of the Bronx, when you were four?"

She pulled something from her pocket that looked like a key, but the head was the size of a man's watch and had a digital screen. She inserted it and after a couple of seconds the door opened with a soft click. We stepped inside and closed the door behind us.

I listened, smelled and probed the house with my senses. Then I leaned close to Gallin's ear and whispered, "If you must know, I went to the Phillips Exeter Academy, an elite boarding school in New Hampshire, founded in the 1700s." I stood erect and straightened my lapels. "Many presidents, senators, writers, judges and significant figures of American society have been alumni of that school."

I saw her eyes, slightly luminous, gazing at me without expression, just a few inches from mine. I prodded her and she crossed the hall to the living room on the right.

The light from the streetlamps outside filtered in through the large window. It was a spacious, attractive living room-cum-dining room with a big marble fireplace and well-used, comfortable furniture. At the far end of the room you could make out the big dining table and the narrow luminescence of the French windows that led out to the lawn. I said:

"She left without closing the drapes."

She gave a soft grunt. "If she left."

"It's been warm and damp all day, Gallin. I smell fried onions, Bolognese sauce, rain and grass, but I don't smell Pamela Peach-Plum or her remains."

In the kitchen the dishwasher was half open and half full with pots and pans, plates and cutlery. Gallin made a point of checking and they all contained traces of spaghetti Bolognese. "Your years at the Phillips Exeter Academy were not wasted, Mason," she said, and checked the door. It was locked and bolted on the inside.

We climbed the stairs and found all the bedrooms empty.

In the master bedroom the bed was unmade, there were clothes on the floor and the wardrobe was open. But there were no signs of a search.

"There was nobody here looking for Saul's work," I said.

Gallin nodded once. "But she was expecting them to come. She was in a hurry,"

We went down to her study, closed the drapes and put on the lights, and spent a couple of hours going through every paper in the room. There was not a trace of Saul Epstein's work. We took possession of all her external drives and her desktop PC. Then I called Sir John.

"My dear chap, how nice to hear from you. Foolish of me not to make it clear it is inadvisable to call me..."

"You made it perfectly clear, Sir John. It's just there is a decision to be made and only you can make it."

"Indeed. A decision to be made..."

"My grandmother always used to say, he who washes his hands, doesn't get to lick the jam off them. So here's your chance to lick the jam. We have the hard drive and all the external drives from Pamela Peach-Plum's private office in her house. You probably know she's gone missing."

"Yes..."

"So, do we take this stuff to the Mossad for them to process it forensically, or would you like it? I could send it to the States but that means delays."

"No, no, no..."

"See? He who washes his hands..."

"Yes, I do understand the metaphor, Mr. Mason. If you'll wait there I'll have a man drop by and collect the stuff."

"You're welcome."

"Yes, ah, and of course, thank you."

We carried the stuff down to the living room and sat in the dark, looking out the big bay window at the quiet street outside. After a while I said, "She heard about Epstein's murder and bolted, but she took care to erase any trace of his work from her office. If she left this stuff here, there is nothing on it either."

"Agreed."

"So, *if* she has it, she's taken his research wherever she's gone. Or she's hidden it in a safe or a bank vault, a PO box—something like that."

"Mm-hmm."

"Million-dollar question, where has she gone?"

"You can stay at my place."

"What?"

"I'm not mad at you anymore. You can stay at my place. Do you prefer not to?"

"No, I do—don't—double negative—that would be great, sure..."

"She probably borrowed a friend's cottage in the country. Same guy she had spaghetti with."

"Oh, OK."

Outside a big SUV pulled up and stopped by the front door.

# FIVE

We handed over the material and received a receipt for it which was about as much use as a stripper in a thong at a vicar's tea party. When the SUV had departed Gallin slapped me on the shoulder and said, "I'm pooped. Let's go grab a bite and have a sleep. We'll continue in the morning, with Nick Barnes."

We descended the stoop toward my rental Jaguar and, as I went to climb in, my cell rang. The number was withheld.

"Yeah."

It was a woman, English, middle class, educated. "Mr. Alex Mason?"

"Yes—"

"Are you alone?"

I glanced at Gallin and gave her the nod to come closer. "Yeah, why?"

"This is Pamela Peach-Plum."

"I had guessed that much. You have a lot of people very worried."

"That's too bad. I think my life is in danger."

"I'm pretty sure you're right. I figure you already know what happened to Saul."

"Yes, obviously. That's why I bolted."

"We have a lot to talk about. I'd like to help you. How did you get my number?"

A fractional hesitation. "That doesn't matter. The thing is I am not sure I trust you."

"Yeah, I can understand that. The trouble is, you haven't got a lot of time, and even fewer options. Whoever did this to Saul looks like a real pro. If he is, he will know how to find you." I lowered my voice. "Just ten minutes ago my partner told me, 'She's probably staying in a friend's cottage in the country. The same guy she had spaghetti Bolognese with last night.' Who was that, Pamela, Sean Noon? How accurate was she?"

She was quiet for a long moment, then she said, "Too accurate."

"How long do you think it would take us to check the properties registered to Sean Noon and find his country cottage?"

"You've made your point."

"Good, I work for the Pentagon, Pamela, in a department that cooperates with the British government. My partner is with your MI5. Believe me, you are a damn sight better off with us than with anybody else who might be looking for you."

"Hobson's choice."

"Not really. We are here to help you and protect you, and to find out what happened to Saul. But we can only do that if you work with us."

There was a long silence. After a moment she seemed to break into fervent prayer: "Oh, Lord, help me in this time of travail! Guide my heart and my steps. All right! You had better come here, but please, *please* don't let anyone follow you!"

"We won't. Where are you?"

"Helston, in Cornwall." I glanced at Gallin. She shrugged and shook her head. I said, "What's that near?"

"It's fifteen miles beyond Truro, on Mounts Bay. If you're in London, it will take you about six or seven hours to get here. Can I WhatsApp you my location safely at the number I am calling now?"

I told her she could. "We'll set out now. We should get to you by three or four in the morning."

When I hung up Gallin said, "What about Nick Barnes?"

"We'll call him in the morning. This is a mess." I gestured at the house. "Why has nobody been here? Why is nobody tracing her?"

She frowned. "How'd you know it was Sean Noon?"

I told her with my face I was surprised she hadn't got it too. "He was working far too hard to show us he didn't believe there was anything to Saul's crazy documentary, while at the same time telling us Helen was beguiled by Saul, but didn't actually know anything herself. He was trying real hard to put everything onto Saul, who was dead anyway, and stress that he and Helen knew nothing. You know, like the witness who tells the killer, 'I haven't seen your face, and if I have I don't remember, and I'm blind anyway.'"

"You got all that? From two minutes talking to him?"

"Well, I grant you I may have jumped the gun, but there

was the, you know: 'She was really excited, Watergate, blah blah, but *he* was the one who knew everything—and he's dead. *She* just went by what *he* told her.' Then there was the, 'Quite honestly, it sounded like science fiction. *Nobody would take it seriously,*' and, 'I thought they'd both taken leave of their senses,' and, when you asked if he could remember any details, 'Yes, but I didn't believe it was real. It was *too ridiculous,*' followed by, referring to FUCCIT, 'I have to say I have never heard of them.' And finally, 'Then Saul showed up dead. But knowing Saul, it was probably some jealous husband, or one of his many women!' But my personal favorite was when he was asked where the work was. He went the color of wax and stammered 'Saul' twice: 'Oh, oh, um, Saul. Saul would have held on to that. Definitely, I think. Almost certainly, for sure.'"

"OK, I hear you."

"They had spaghetti last night. She scared the bejaysus out of him, he likes her, maybe a lot, so he gives her the key to his cottage in Cornwall and when we come around, he doesn't know who the hell we are—we might be killers for all he knows—so he tries to cover himself and keep her in the clear while he's at it. Then he calls her and tells her we were there."

"OK—"

"But it doesn't tell us, Gallin, why her fears were unfounded. Why has nobody been there? Why wasn't the place ransacked? And why is nobody tracing her?"

IT WAS A LONG, tiring drive. We took the freeway as far as Basingstoke, and came off onto the A303, a two-lane road that plunged us immediately into dark countryside, cutting through small, sleeping hamlets and villages, skirting thatched cottages set back from the road among black woodlands and shadowy hedged gardens. We passed Dummer which was, perhaps appropriately, right next to Nutley, and moved on west, going into ever more remote countryside. Here the ancient, ink-black hills of Wiltshire rose against a translucent night sky, topped by the eerie stencils of oaks and poplars, like secret funeral processions of the night.

After about three hours the road had become single lane and it felt like we were lost in the middle of nowhere. My eyes were getting heavy and I turned to Gallin.

"You want to take over? I figure we're about halfway."

She nodded. "Sure."

I pulled over onto the entrance to a dirt track, put the car in neutral and climbed out. The moon was rising in a fat, orange glow over woodland in the west, and I stopped a moment to look at it. Gallin came around the trunk of the car and leaned on me. Then she tucked her head under my elbow and put her arms around my chest and squeezed. "Great lummox," she said, and then, "Look," and she pointed north, slightly to the left of the moon. It was hard to make out, but about a dozen tall shadows stood on a small rise. They were strange, "other" and slightly frightening, like they were shades watching us. We watched them back a while as the moon rose and touched them with a strange, metallic light.

"What are they?" I asked.

She looked up at me and smiled. "Stonehenge," she whispered. "Where the Druids learned how to die."

We stood a little longer, then, shuddering in the chill air, we got back in the car and continued west. The roads were virtually empty and we made good time, speeding past tiny villages that emerged suddenly from the trees with weird names like Upottery, Honitton and Gittisham, until we started to climb at last into the Black Hills, and entered the home stretch toward Mount Bay, flung out on the farthest extreme of England, out in the wild, North Atlantic Ocean.

By the time we arrived in Helston it was four AM and the moon was rising toward its zenith. We entered the town from the north, along a road that was so overgrown with hedges and chestnut trees, you thought you were still out in the countryside. Until you found you suddenly were actually in the center of the town.

The center of town consisted of one, two and three-storey stone buildings that were probably between four and five hundred years old. It was deadly quiet and deeply asleep as we passed through it: the windows were like blind eyes focused on dense shadows like dark dreams.

We turned down into Wendron Street, empty and silent, passed the tiny, blue Flora's Cinema beside the Helston Meadery, and we were suddenly out of town again, on the Porthleven Road, among thick forest crowding in on either side. The moon-glow of a small lake slid by on the right and then the GPS, projecting its luminous map over Gallin's face in the darkness of the cab, told us to turn down a narrow track that took us still deeper in among the trees.

We rolled and lurched for a couple of minutes, following the ineffectual glow of the headlamps, and suddenly we were there, outside a dry stone wall with a picket gate that gave onto a front yard with rosebushes and a small lawn. A stone path led to the arched, oak door of a stone cottage with two floors and a thatched roof. On the right there was a gravel driveway and a parking lot in back.

We pulled in and the soft crunch of the gravel sounded loud in the predawn hush. The engine and the lights died and we climbed out of the car into the hush. A mile or two away to the south you could just make out the wink of the moon on the black ocean. The house loomed dark and silent. Above it the chimneypot half-concealed the moon.

Gallin stood by the hood of the car. Her training told her we should not be close. I looked at her and we both listened for breathing. I gave a small nod which she returned almost imperceptibly. I said, "I'll check the front," and took a noisy step forward while she moved silently up to the fence. She had her Sig in her hand and I wrenched open the gate, pulling my own P226 from under my arm as Gallin snapped, "Freeze!"

The woman was hunkered down, staring at me with enormous eyes and trying hard not to cry. She was holding a huge kitchen knife in both hands and at that moment it was pointing a little unsteadily at my lower belly.

I smiled at her. "Pamela?"

She half-rasped and half-whispered, "Are you...? Who are you?"

"That depends on whether you are Pamela. If you are, I am Alex Mason and this is Captain Aila Gallin, and we are your new best friends." I leaned forward with a nasty glint in my eye. "But if you're not, I am probably your worst nightmare." The more scared she looked, the more dangerous she looked. So I cut the funny act and tried for reassuring instead. "However, I am going to go out on a limb and say you *are* probably Pamela Peach-Plum. Am I right?"

"Yes," she said, looking no less terrified.

"OK, Pamela, I am going to put my weapon away, and I would like you to hand me that knife, handle first. And please do bear in mind that if you try to stab me Captain Gallin will shoot you, and we don't want that to happen, do we? Do you understand that?"

She nodded and hesitated. "You're American, aren't you?"

"As mom's apple pie."

She stood, handed me the knife, straightened her clothes and arched an eyebrow at Gallin. "You must be exhausted after your drive. I can offer you coffee and perhaps some breakfast?"

Gallin smiled gratitude at her and put her piece away, and we followed her into the big farmhouse kitchen where, after a brief hesitation, she flipped the switch. "I suppose it's safe?"

I shrugged. "Nobody followed us."

There were yellow gingham drapes closed across the window above the sink. Beside the sink there was a modern, electric stove, and beside that a big old iron range. In the middle of the floor there was a farmhouse table with an empty fruit bowl in the middle, and a rough wooden door stood closed in the far wall.

Gallin dropped into a chair at the table and I leaned with my hands on the back of another, watching Pamela. Now that she wasn't terrified, she came across as a handsome, intelligent woman. She was in hr early fifties and to many men she would be attractive.

She unscrewed the mocha percolator and started pouring water in it. I said:

"Tell me about Saul."

She spooned coffee into the hopper and tamped it down.

"Saul was that most special of things, a real ace journalist —and I do mean ace. He was everything a top journalist should be, an idealist who truly believed in his ideals, and in the people's right to know what was happening to them and their society. I always had a feeling, from the time I first met him, that he would one day give his life in the service of one of his stories. And in the end he did."

Gallin said, "We don't know that to be the case yet. Do you?"

She was screwing the top of the coffee pot back on, but paused, staring down at it in her hands. She shook her head.

"Know? No, I don't *know*, but I'd be damned surprised if that wasn't what happened. If Saul had you in his sights, you were in serious trouble. And if his story was going to cause as much trouble as he said it would, some very, *very* powerful people were going to get badly hurt. My hunch is that he finally went too far. I'm going to miss him."

She put the pot on the stove and turned it on. The ring glowed red. I frowned. "Were you close?"

It started as a sad laugh and ended up as a sigh. "Good journalists don't get close. They have allies. I was his ally. I respected him. I was probably in love with him at some point, when we were younger. That's about as far as it went."

"You said your hunch was that he finally went too far. Can you be more precise?"

"Saul was extremely jealous about his work, and very secretive. Over the years he and I had come to an under-standing. Saul gave me a thumbnail sketch of whatever his project was and, in theory at least, I either approved it or I didn't. In fact I always approved it because he was a real pro, and by the time he brought me a proposal he had already done enough work to show it was viable. After that I would not hear much from him until the project was ready to produce." She paused, her gaze lost among her thoughts. "We'd been doing that for a long time, and we'd produced one red-hot controversy after another. Our ratings were sky-high. But his facts were always rock solid, we never once— *never once*—got sued and he made a fortune for the production company."

I shrugged. "OK, I think we knew that much. So how did he go too far on this story?"

She moved from the stove to the fridge, opened it and pulled out bacon and eggs. From the bread bin she took a loaf of bread. Finally, as she cut into the loaf, she said:

"Nobody except him knew. The last thing *I* knew, he called me and told me he had the greatest story in the history of journalism. Nobody would believe it, except that he had the proof—rock-solid proof. This was going to shake the Western world to its roots, but he feared for his life."

"Did he tell the police any of this?"

She smiled for the first time and dropped the bread in the toaster. "Yeah, well... The police are employees, Mr. Mason, and you never *really* know who they work for. So we never really involved them in our investigations." Then, more seriously, she added, "I asked him if he wanted to pull the plug. I was thinking if his life was at risk, so was mine. But he said he didn't. He said we had a duty to the people, and the story was too big not to tell."

She started peeling rashers of bacon from the pack and

laying them in the pan. They hissed and the rich smell filled the kitchen, along with the dark aroma of the coffee. Gallin stood and went to the fridge. She pulled out the butter and said, "So where is it?"

Pamela glanced at her, then broke eggs into a bowl and started whisking them with salt and pepper. "I'm useless at fried eggs. You get them scrambled. Where's what?"

"The story," said Gallin. "Where is it?"

"I have no idea."

"I don't buy that. You're the only person he would have entrusted it to. You must have it."

She gave a small, incredulous laugh. "And not use it? Not broadcast it? In the wake of his murder? Do you know what the ratings would be on that show? Forgive me, but you're out of your mind. The person who has the story, is the person who killed Saul. I should have thought that was obvious."

Gallin had pulled the toast out of the toaster and was buttering it, setting it out on plates. I said, "I don't know that you didn't kill Saul, Pamela."

She turned to stare at me a moment, then started sharing out bacon onto two plates.

"I suppose not. It's not very likely though, is it?"

"I don't know yet. You must have a theory, a hunch, some idea... You said yourself the whole process started with him outlining his project for you. Yet you're cagey, subtly obstructive. Why?"

Gallin dropped the toast on the plates and brought over the coffee and the cups while Pamela dished out the eggs with the bacon. The combination of smells was intoxicating in the early hours on an empty stomach.

Pamela sat and watched us a moment while we ate. After a moment she said, "It goes against the grain to help government agents. It's become an instinct." She watched us a moment longer, then started talking.

"He had this idea he'd been nursing for a few years. It sounds like science fiction and for a long time I refused to touch it. His show—our show—was highly respected and viewed by everyone from McDonald's drones to Harvard academics." She shook her head. "If I started rocking the boat with wild conspiracy theories, we were going to kill the goose and break the eggs, and we weren't even going to get a damn omelet out of it. Both our careers would be finished."

I wiped my mouth. "What was the idea?"

"He believed there was an elite, composed of Anglophone billionaires—"

Gallin screwed up her brow. "Of *what?*"

"Billionaires from the USA, Britain, Canada, Australia, New Zealand, South Africa and Israel."

"Israel is Anglophone now?"

"Eighty-five percent of Israelis speak English." She recited it like it was a fact she was tired of hearing. "One hundred percent of the Israeli elite speak English. There are seventy-one billionaires in Israel, which is probably the highest per-capita rate in the world. America has over seven hundred billionaires, and thirty percent of them are Jewish."

Gallin sighed noisily. "Is this the old Semitic Plot to Rule the World fantasy rehashed? Because let me tell you, sister, the Brits and the Americans, not to mention the Vatican, the French and the Germans, have not been shy about trying to rule the world!"

"It's nothing to do with that. Saul Epstein was Jewish, remember? The name kind of hints at it."

"Fine, keep going."

"He believed there was an elite. Eligibility to join the club was dependent on just three factors: you must speak English as your first language, you must be white Caucasian or Jewish, and you must be a billionaire. Those three criteria make you eligible, but to become a member there is a fourth criterion, and that is absolute fidelity."

Gallin was shaking her head. She looked vaguely nauseated. "It's science fiction. He'd lost the plot."

I turned to her with my lower lip shoved out to show I didn't agree. "You," I said, "of all people, as a Jew and an Israeli, should know that membership of a special club—whether it's a religion, a priesthood, an aristocracy or political movement—can drive people crazy to the point of believing themselves superior..." I turned to Pamela and added, "and with the right of life and death over entire races."

Pamela nodded and glanced at Gallin, who was rubbing her face with her palms. "The Third Reich and Islam tell us that much," she turned back to me, "but this went further..." She paused, looking down at her hands. "...goes further. What Saul believed, and claimed that he had proved, was that they had some kind of program of genetic engineering going on, using nano-technology to alter the genetic coding at a molecular or even atomic level, to lengthen lifespans, create immunities, heighten performance..."

She went quiet. It was probably just seconds, but it seemed longer. Gallin spoke softly into the silence, "Let us make man in our image, after our likeness: and let them have dominion over the fish of the sea, and over the fowl of the air, and over the cattle, and over all the earth..." She met Pamela's gaze and added, "Only now it is Man making himself in God's image."

I drained my coffee and set down the cup. It sounded loud in the quiet kitchen. Outside a streak of pale gray reached up into the sky over the hedgerows.

"He claimed he had proved this?"

She shook her head. Gallin frowned. "He hadn't?"

Pamela said, "He had proved it conclusively, beyond a shadow of a doubt. That's what he said. Beyond any doubt at all. But the problem, what outraged him, was what was in store for the rest of us. The cull."

# SIX

Gallin stood and walked to the sink. She leaned on it looking out at the inky stencils of the trees against the paling sky. After a while she spoke in a disembodied voice.

"Saul Epstein might have been many things, but one thing he wasn't was stupid. He knew the risk he was facing, and he knew the danger he was putting you in too, not to mention his ex-wife." She turned, leaning her ass against the sink and crossing her arms. "Knowing who he was up against, there was no way he was going to make it simple to get ahold of his work." She shrugged and gave a small, incredulous laugh. "Turn up, ring at the door, shoot him in the head, collect up his material and walk away. I don't believe it. If he was aware how powerful his opponents were, he would not have been that careless, or downright stupid."

Pamela was staring at the table. "I'd have to agree, on the face of it."

Gallin pressed her. "The obvious thing for him to do would have been to put the stuff in your care."

Pamela didn't look up. "So maybe that's why he didn't do it. If he had, I would certainly be dead by now."

I said quietly, "In that case, what *did* he do?"

Her voice was barely a whisper. "I don't know."

I sighed. "I'll tell you what I think, Pamela. I agree with Captain Gallin. I think Saul was too smart by half to allow the investigation of his life, his magnum opus, to be stolen from him. I think he had a plan, I think he made provision for his own death and made sure his work was safe."

She still wouldn't look at me. "Maybe you're right."

Gallin snapped, "Pamela, I need you to get your head out of your ass and face up to this. If this organization exists, and if they are as powerful and batshit crazy as Saul thought they were, you are as good as dead anyway because you will be number one on their hit list of loose ends. You have one option, and that's to come out fighting and accept our protection. But you need to *react! Now!*"

She finally raised her eyes and looked at Gallin. "And do what?"

Gallin thrust out her hand and pointed at her. "You *know* where he has put his research. And if you don't know, you have a pretty good idea what he's done with it. You have to quit acting out of fear and *talk* to us! Tell us what you think and what you suspect! You think you're any safer hiding here and hinting at stuff than you would be in London or Washington talking to us and helping us to break this cabal? You're out of your mind."

She didn't answer. She sat staring at the tabletop. I pulled my cell from my pocket and called Nero.

"What?"

"I am here with Saul Epstein's producer."

"And?"

"We're in a remote village in Cornwall, where she is in hiding."

"From whom?"

"From an Anglophone cabal who want to remake themselves in God's image using nano-technology and genetic engineering. They also want to depopulate the world in the process. It sounds like science fiction to me, but Saul Epstein claimed to have proved it conclusively."

"It is no more science fiction than the German death camps were. She claims Saul had proved it?"

I glanced at her and repeated her words. "Conclusively, beyond any doubt at all."

"Who has his work?"

"We don't know yet."

"Find it. Bring her to me. I'll have a plane waiting for you...." He trailed off. After half a minute he came back. "Go to Corsham, in Wiltshire, stay at the Guyers House Hotel. It's remote and secluded. Remember to bring luggage. People traveling without luggage get noticed. I will arrange a flight out of Sheldon Airfield outside Chippenham. I'll be in touch."

As I hung up Gallin was shaking her head. "I need a couple of hours' sleep."

I nodded. "I'll keep watch. Pack three cases or bags. People traveling without bags get noticed. We'll head out at six. I'll sleep in the car."

They bedded down in a room upstairs that was inaccessible from anywhere except the stairs. The front door of the cottage was solid oak and had two big, old-fashioned iron deadbolts, one at the top and one at the bottom. Access to the house would have to be either through the living-room window, which would be awkward and noisy, or through the kitchen door. Anyone who tried either would be dead before breakfast.

I made another pot of coffee and kept myself awake by trying to decide whether Saul Epstein had been killed by a jealous woman or by a hit man, hired because he, Saul, was such a dangerous investigative journalist. Then I thought, if you're going to have an untimely death, that had to be about as good as an untimely death gets. I had a vision of them all standing around in purgatory, drinking coffee and eating biscuits:

"How did *your* untimely death come about, Phil? I was trying to swat a wasp in my car and drove into a truck."

"Man! Sucks! How about you, Danny?"

"Oh, I was changing a tile on the roof and slipped and broke my neck. How about you, Pete?"

"Me? I choked on a lima bean. What about you, Saul?"

A self-deprecating smile and, "They're still investigating. It might have been my supermodel girlfriend who shot me because she was jealous of my PhD ex-wife, or it might have been an international organization terrified of the exposé I was about to broadcast to the world..."

Pretty cool.

Also improbable. The word was *improbable*. But then Saul himself was improbable. And whichever way you looked at it, there didn't seem to be a probable explanation that covered all the facts.

That kind of nonsense got me to five forty, when I

made more coffee and started preparing breakfast. At five fifty Gallin came down looking like she'd just slept twelve hours. Pamela was close behind her, yawning and rubbing her eyes.

Outside, it wasn't so much a dawn chorus as hell and pandemonium breaking loose among rioting starlings. In the east, the sun was bleeding red onto the horizon. Above, puffy, watercolor clouds were breaking to reveal patches of pale, fresh blue sky against which poplars, oaks, sycamores, willows and chestnuts loomed tall and dark.

It was a five-hour drive. Gallin drove, but I didn't sleep. The rain had eased off and the early, patchy sun gleamed on the wet blacktop, giving it at times a steel blue sheen. Under the patches of blue overhead, when you could see to left or right through the huge hedgerows, the waterlogged fields rolled away among an endless patchwork of more hedgerows and woodlands, gleaming under the armada of billowing white clouds above.

We didn't talk beyond the usual, "Let's stop for coffee at the next gas station," kind of comment. Gallin's unanswered question from the night before remained unanswered, which of itself spoke volumes, but my instinct told me to let it lie until we reached the hotel.

We did that at shortly after eleven AM. We entered Corsham from the southeast along the A7 Bath Road and pretty soon we came to Guyers Lane on the left, between a bunch of trees, and a broad field of corn on the right. As we turned in I heard Pamela take a deep breath in the back of the car and blow out through puffed cheeks. Gallin spun the wheel into the hotel drive and rolled along a dirt track shaded by giant oaks, chestnuts and walnut trees. A bend in the drive led to a large, gravel parking lot. There, she killed the engine and turned to look at Pamela.

"You ready to answer me yet?"

She nodded. "Yeah, I guess I haven't much choice."

"Good, we'll check in and get some coffee and sandwiches. We'll talk over coffee."

Reception was in a quaint lounge which had probably once been the manor house kitchen. There was an iron stove in the wall, some IKEA sofas against the walls and exposed beams on the ceiling. The receptionist was a cute redhead with an accent that might have been German, except it was mellow and didn't make you feel you were about to be interrogated. She smiled and handed me an old Chubb key.

"Ve heff the Superior Room for you and your vife, ent room five for your sister." She pointed toward the dining room. "First door on ze left and up ze stairs. Enjoy! Anyssing you want, you just ask."

The stairs creaked all the way up. Gallin went with Pamela to her room and I went into the Superior Room on my own. There was a large, four-poster bed, a view of the parking lot and a bucket of ice containing a bottle of Pol Roger. I wondered vaguely what kind of story Nero had spun for the benefit of the staff. He was a great believer in minute details. He figured a loving couple with a spinster sister would attract less attention and be more forgettable than an odd assortment of one man and two women traveling with practically no luggage.

I left the room and climbed the stairs to room five. I knocked and Gallin opened the door, standing back to let me in. I went in and she sat on the bed. It wasn't a four-poster. I could hear the shower going in the en suite.

I said, "We have to drink a bottle of champagne, have wild, passionate sex and leave our four-poster bed in a tangle of twisted sheets."

She blinked a couple of times without expression. "I was planning on waxing my legs. Can it wait?"

I shook my head. "It has to be now. I can handle the stubble."

She arched an eyebrow. "You're funny, deep down funny, where it's not like funny anymore."

"Nero got us a bottle of Pol Roger on ice, and a four-poster bed. The staff are going to wonder why we didn't make use of them."

"I'll tell them it was your war wound. Tragic, so young, handsome, intelligent, yet deprived of his manhood in a bizarre accident involving a Baghdad Hilton ashtray and a ferret..."

"I'm serious."

"You're serious. You expect me to surrender my virginity to you so the hotel staff won't talk..."

I frowned. She stood and left the room, muttering, "Keep an eye on sis."

I stretched out on the bed with a slight feeling of unease, staring at the heavy, exposed beams on the ceiling. The sound of the shower stopped and after a moment Pamela stepped out, wrapped in a towel. She stopped dead and said, "Oh!"

I sat up and smiled. "Sorry, Captain Gallin had to step out for a moment."

The words were fresh out of my mouth when Gallin's voice rose through the floorboards, urgently repeating the word, "Yes!" Then there was an inarticulate noise reminiscent of trying to move a very heavy object. There followed finally an embarrassing series of groans which I felt pretty sure would elevate me to legendary status among the staff of Guyers House Hotel for some time to come.

When the noises had died down, Pamela muttered, "I'll just get dressed," and returned to the bathroom with a fistful of clothes. A moment later Gallin came in and frowned at me.

"You're good. I left you half the bottle. You'd better go get it while it's cold. And have a shower. You need it."

At the door I paused and looked back. "I know this means nothing to you and you'll move on, but it means everything to me. I will never forget…"

"Get the hell out of here, Mason. Go order some food in the bar."

We met in the bar fifteen minutes later. It had wooden floors and wooden paneled walls, leather chairs and old prints on the walls, of sailing ships and generals from the Raj. I'd ordered a plate of sandwiches and a pot of coffee. Now we were seated around a mahogany table, Gallin poured coffee and Pamela stared out the door at the damp day outside.

"Saul had a nose," she said suddenly. "He had a kind of sixth sense. He'd start teasing and ferreting, and scratching away, and sooner or later he would find it. He just *knew*. It was about three months ago, I suppose. He had become obsessed with the Foundation story…"

"FUCCIT—Just Do It," Gallin interposed as she took a sandwich.

"Yes. I knew what he was like so I finally yielded. I told him to go for it. If he was that sure, there had to be something in it. And that was pretty much the last I heard from him."

Gallin had been listening carefully, chewing slowly. "What happened?"

Pamela picked up a sandwich and looked at it for a moment, then set it down on her plate.

"He called me. It must have been a couple of weeks ago. He said he was very excited about the story. It was his best work ever." She picked up her sandwich, put it down again and sipped coffee instead. "His best work ever. He was on the top line, talking about rocking the establishment, constitutional change to bring the military-industrial complex under Congressional control, repealing the National Security Act. It was crazy talk, but then, Saul wasn't crazy. He was a hard-headed realist."

I frowned. "Wait a minute. He had got that far in just three months? An investigation that deep would take years."

She nodded at her plate, then shrugged. "You've seen Saul's show. Who hasn't? He was meticulous to the point of neurosis. If he made a statement it was because he had proved it several times over. He destroyed a dozen reputations, but he was never once sued for libel. Never." She shrugged again. "But he said he was wrapping it up, and the effect would be cataclysmic. That was the word he used. Cataclysmic."

Gallin spread her hands and said, with some emphasis, "So what happened?"

"I told him to bring it in and let me see it."

"So you *did* see it!"

"Wait, let me finish. I told him to let me see it, and that was when he told me he thought there might be a contract out on him. That was the last time we spoke. The next thing I heard, he'd been found murdered. I panicked and bolted."

Gallin bit into a sandwich and spoke around it as she chewed. "That's quite a story, Pamela. But it doesn't tell us much more than we knew already. And it doesn't answer the question, where do you think he put his work for safekeeping? Now, I am going to ask you again. If he didn't give them to you, who else would he trust enough..."

"There was a guy he'd worked with a lot over the years. As I keep telling you, Saul was not *close* to anyone, not even Julia. But there were people he respected and there were people he trusted more than others. He probably trusted me more than most. And in as much as he trusted anyone, he trusted Nick. Nick is a corporate lawyer in an Anglo-American firm. He specializes in intellectual property and Saul relied a lot on his advice. It's possible, just possible he put it in his care."

I nodded. "Nick Barnes."

She glanced at me, a little surprised. "Yes, Nick Barnes. You've come across him?"

"His name popped up."

She half-nodded upward and her eyes drifted to the open door. Outside it had started drizzling. "Milgram Smith and Rapaport," she said. "Red Lion Square, in Holborn."

# SEVEN

I STEPPED OUT INTO THE DRIZZLE, DIALED THE
number for Milgram Smith and Rapaport. While it rang I
strolled out of the small courtyard and round to the lawn
and the pond, with small drops of water accumulating on
my scalp and running down the back of my neck. I found
the shelter of a walnut tree beside the pond just as a brisk
female voice said, "Milgram Smith and Rapaport," faster
than you'd think possible, and then added, "How can I help
you?"

"I want to talk to Nick Barnes."

"Have you got his extension number?"

I tried and failed to put a smile in my voice. "If I had, I
wouldn't have called you. I am calling from the Pentagon's
Office of the Director of Intelligence and I need to talk to
Mr. Barnes. Can you put me through, please?"

Her voice was replaced by a ringing sound and a male
voice said, "Personnel, can I help you?"

"I hope so. My name is Mason, I am calling from the

Pentagon's Office of the Director of Intelligence, and I need to talk to Nick Barnes. He is an attorney—a solicitor—at your firm."

"Bear with me, Mr. Mason..." I was about to stop bearing when he came on the line again and said, "Hold please..." and it rang twice before a South African woman answered. You could tell she was South African because she rolled her Rs, sounded all the silent Hs and used vowels that don't really exist. She said, "Mr. Mason? This is Ava van Niekirk. Why do you want to talk to Mr. Barnes?" I raised my face to the drizzle, getting a grip on my fading patience, but before I could tell her it was none of her damned business, she said, "If you don't mind me asking?"

"I don't mind you asking, Ms. van Niekirk, but I am not going to answer your question. Perhaps you'd like to tell me why instead of speaking to Mr. Barnes, I am speaking to you?"

"Can you give me some identification? Office of the Director of Intelligence is quite a claim."

"I am not sure what your problem is, Ms. van Niekirk. I can claim to be Mickey Mouse if I want to. I just want to talk to Mr. Barnes."

She took a moment to reply, and when she did she said, "Mr. Barnes doesn't work here anymore. He handed in his resignation a couple of weeks ago and left just this morning."

He'd told us to be punctual, that he was travelling. I had several options open to me. I didn't take any of them. Instead I waited for her to fill the silence. Finally she said, "Nick was in my department, Intellectual Property. That's why you were put through to me. Can I help you in any way?"

I was about to tell her she couldn't, but instead I said, "I don't know. He handed in his resignation two weeks ago?"

"Yuz."

Something else had happened two weeks ago. What? Epstein. He had called Pamela to say he'd finished his research. "Where'd he go?"

"New York. He is moving to a Manhattan firm who had headhunted him. Is he in some kind of trouble?"

"We just want to ask him a few questions. Ms. van Niekirk, did you ever have joint conferences with Nick?"

"Sometimes. They are covered by privilege."

"Yeah, I know. Just before he left, did an old friend come to see him about a TV show?"

She left it just long enough to signal me I was right before she said, "I can't answer that, Mr. Mason. You'd have to talk to Nick."

"Can you give me a contact number?"

"He is going to work for Trans Atlantic Legal Services, 112 White Street. They have the two top floors. You had better approach them."

I hung up and called Nero.

"Stop calling me. You report to Sir John. Call him."

"No. Listen, I need Nick Barnes' address and where-abouts. He left Milgram Smith and Rapaport to move to Trans Atlantic Legal Services, 112 White Street, in Manhattan. He takes up his new post in a couple of weeks. Meantime, where is he? I need to talk to him yesterday morning. By the way, did you arrange a flight for Pamela?"

"I'm waiting for confirmation. Will you be on that flight?"

"Yes. How long have we got?"

"A few hours. Hold on..." He went quiet for a while. Then I heard him snapping, "I need an answer now, dammit!" Then he came back on the line. "One AM in the morning. That is, tonight."

"I get it. Tonight. One AM. Where?"

"I'll have the pilot send you the location. Will Captain Gallin be accompanying you?"

"Yes."

He sighed noisily. "The investigation is in the United Kingdom, Alex. Do not get sidetracked."

"Right. Please get me Nick Barnes' whereabouts."

"You teeter on the edge of insolence at times, Alex."

"No, sir. It's these transatlantic calls, they..." I made some childish crackling noises into the phone and hung up. Then squelched across the lawn and entered the hotel again through the dining room. After that I got lost in a maze of creaking corridors and eventually asked a cute waitress with a sweet voice and big black eyes to point me in the direction of the bar.

Gallin was there drinking a pint of English beer. Pamela had that enduring symbol of Woke, a plastic bottle of mineral water in front of her and kept screwing and unscrewing the pale-blue cap. I sat and pointed at the bottle. "Do you know how many dolphins have died because of those bottles?"

Her eyes went wide and she pushed the bottle away from her. I had no idea either, but she didn't know that. I hailed the girl behind the bar and said, "Let me have another round of sandwiches, and a couple of dry martinis here."

I looked at Gallin. She was staring at me like I was talking and she was listening carefully. We sat like that for a long moment: Pamela looking unhappily at her disgusting plastic bottle of water, Gallin listening attentively to my silence and me staring at her and thinking. Finally I said, "Nick Barnes is in New York. You can come with me and talk to him, or you can get to work on the Foundation for Computers yadda yadda."

"Thanks."

I wagged my finger at her. The waitress brought the martinis and I had to wait till she'd gone before I wagged my finger again. "You know what worries me?"

"The effect of small plastic bottles on the global dolphin population?"

"What worries me, is that he wasn't tortured."

Gallin had her glass halfway to her mouth but stopped and put it slowly down again. Pamela was frowning at me. But as she drew breath her face cleared and she sank back in her chair.

"Oh..." she said.

And as though the phoneme had opened some secret tap in the sky, the heavens opened and a gray mist of water fell, raising a noisy hiss in the gardens outside.

A little later the sandwiches arrived and we ate them in silence, watching the rain, until Pamela drained her glass and said, "I need to get some sleep."

I nodded and we all went up together. Gallin went with Pamela, and I crashed alone on the four-poster bed.

Irony.

The rain spattered on the leaded window. Through it I could see the trees tossing and swaying in the rain.

A close friend.

Is getting shot by a close friend ironic? With friends like

that, who needs enemies? The doorbell rings, he goes and opens the door. *His work is not in his office.* The reason is *not,* as everybody assumed without thinking, that it was stolen by his killer. Because A, Saul is too damned smart to have it lying around for the killer to steal, and B, *two weeks* had transpired since he told Pamela he'd finished it. Besides, Simon the janitor had told us it was not there. No, it isn't there because he has put it into safekeeping somewhere.

But if the killer has come and rung at the door to kill Saul and take the work, then why does he not torture Saul first to find out where it is? *Why did he not torture Saul?*

There was only one possible answer. I closed my eyes and drifted toward sleep.

Because he already knew. Because he already had it.

I was suddenly awake and it was dark outside. I could still hear the patter of the rain, and there was a wet glimmer through the window. I sat up and checked my phone. It was three minutes after six PM. There were no messages. I frowned and scratched my head. It felt later, but I could hear voices outside.

I stood under the shower for five minutes, then shaved and dressed and stepped out onto the landing. It was quiet. I climbed the stairs to Pamela's room. Though I could dimly hear voices downstairs, and the occasional clatter of cutlery, the silence on the stairs seemed total, as though it existed in a bubble, in its own separate reality. I tried to ignore the feeling of discomfort and knocked on her door. I heard Gallin's voice, slightly muffled inside, saying "Hang on!" Then there was a creak behind me. I turned and saw a man on the stairs. He was in his late forties, tweed jacket, reddish hair flecked with gray, clean shaven, tanned.

He nodded briefly and moved away from me along the corridor. I knocked again and Gallin's voice called, "Hang *on!*"

"Oh, um..."

I turned. He had his left hand on his chin and he was frowning as he came toward me. "Mr. Mason?"

He was six or seven feet away from me when I said, "Yes..." Then it played out in slow motion. He took a long step toward me with his right foot and his right hand came up and under with a wicked, seven-inch black blade in it. I recognized the Fairbairn and Sykes as I fell back and the razor point skimmed past my belly. If he'd caught me he would have disemboweled me.

I hit the wall and he kept coming. Instinctively I kicked at his forward knee. It didn't stop him and he slashed at my face. I couldn't back away and grabbed his wrist in both hands. That didn't stop him either. He pounded my ribs three times, hard, in rapid succession with his left fist till I let go his wrist with my right and smashed my elbow into his face.

He staggered back but didn't release the knife. I was wheezing badly and felt faint. He lunged and I grabbed his wrist in both hands again and tried to twist against the joint, but the bastard was strong and I was winded. So I kicked his knee again, twice. He threw a left cross which I took on my shoulder and kicked at his knee again. It was beginning to tell and his eyes were getting wild. So he lunged forward and sunk his teeth into my left wrist. The pain was excruciating. I screamed but suppressed it in my throat so it was inaudible, and used the pain to power three kicks that were more like stamps into his knee until I felt the cartilage crack. Then he fell back, gasping and wide-eyed, and the knife fell to the floor.

My wrist was bleeding badly and my whole right arm was numb. He was still hobbling on his left leg, leaning forward slightly, and still had a look of astonishment on his face. But his right hand was reaching under his jacket. He'd tried for the silent kill. It had failed and he was now going to make a noise. A focused rage gripped me and I stepped forward and kicked savagely at his jaw. As I did it the bedroom door opened and Gallin stepped out, making him look at her. So my foot caught the side of his face and he slumped back, with his Glock halfway out of its holster.

I stooped for the knife but my fingers wouldn't close on the hilt. I saw him pull the weapon free of his jacket and point it at me just as Gallin trod on his hand with her left foot and kicked him in the jaw with her right. His eyes rolled and he fell back.

I picked up the knife with my left hand and slipped it in my boot. I took his right leg in my left arm and she took his left and we dragged him into the room. Pamela was standing in the middle of the floor staring at us. Gallin closed the door and said, "How bad is your hand?"

"It hurts like hell and it's numb."

"Are you incapacitated?"

"No. I need a couple of strong painkillers and a whiskey. I'll be OK."

"I'm asking because he's probably not alone."

"I'm OK. Get me some painkillers. And a shot. You'd better take Pamela down to the dining room. I'll join you in a moment. I want to ask this bastard some questions."

I sat on the bed holding my hand, trying to ignore the

pain, while she went to her toilet bag and brought me a couple of tablets with a miniature bottle of Scotch from the minibar. When I had downed them she said, "You're not going to ask him any questions, tough guy."

I scowled at her as I drained the bottle. "Why?"

"Because dead men don't talk."

"You killed him?"

"He was going to shoot you." She shrugged. "I thought about it. Maybe he could tell me who sent him and why he'd killed you. But what the hell, call me sentimental. I thought I'd rather have you alive."

I sighed. "Thanks."

"Anytime. We lock him in. We go down to dinner. When you get your location for the flight we go out like we're going to look at the rain and we drive to the airfield taking the key with us. By the time they find the body we'll be in New York."

I nodded, photographed his face and took his prints, then sent them to Lovelock in Washington. I got a message back saying, "Send them to the London Office."

I wrote back, "Force of habit. Now you've got them, process them."

I washed my hands, put a sticking plaster over where he'd broken the skin and went back into the bedroom. Gallin had covered the corpse with a blanket, but Pamela was still staring at the shrouded bulk. I took a hold of her shoulders.

"Pamela, you need to get a grip. You know why this man was here?"

She frowned and looked past me at the lump on the floor.

"He was here to find out where Saul's work was, and

then to kill you. Now if we are going to get out of this alive, you need to get a grip and stay cool. Do you understand?"

She studied my face a moment, then nodded slowly. I glanced at Gallin and she opened the door. As we went down the stairs I sent a message to Nero: "Where's the damned plane? We have company at the hotel."

As we entered the dining room the cute waitress with the nice smile and the dark eyes led us to a table and handed us three menus. Gallin took hers and said, "You'd better get us three Jameson's straight up. Make them doubles."

The waitress wrote that down and as she smiled and turned to go, Gallin added, "And we'll have the smoked salmon to start and then the rib-eye steak. No wine, but bring a jug of water."

We sat and Pamela looked unhappily at Gallin. "I don't like steak."

"You need the protein." Her eyes strayed to the door and she added, "And if you don't now, you will by the time we get to New York."

# EIGHT

THE PAIN IN MY ARM WAS NO LONGER CONSTANT. Most of the time it was a background throb, but occasionally it welled into full-blown agony. Gallin laughed like I'd said something witty and leaned forward, shaking her head. "Your three o'clock," she said. I chuckled and leaned in to Pamela. "Laugh or I'll take you outside and shoot you. I mean it. Smile!"

She looked at me like I was insane, and a horrible hybrid of terror and supine obedience twisted into a sickly smile on her face as I turned and pretended to look for the waitress. She was talking to a man at the door. He had that unmistakable military look: the stance, the straight back, the neat crease in his pants. The shoulders of his linen jacket were spattered with rain and he was glancing around the dining room. This was the dead guy's partner. I didn't catch his eye, but he saw us and knew who we were. He turned and left and the waitress went to get our drinks.

Pamela had gone pasty white. "What's happening?"

Gallin said, "How many are there?"

"It's a hit team. Probably ex-Australian or Kiwi SAS."

"Shit. Those guys are hard."

"Ask my hand." I closed my eyes. "Let me think. The hit teams operate in twos. So this is the other half of the guy upstairs. But I am guessing they would have at least two teams on us."

"So three. This guy, probably parked in the parking lot waiting, and a car at the end of the drive to take us out if we get past these two."

I nodded. "Yeah."

The waitress brought our drinks and set them on the table. As she walked away Gallin said, "I've worked with those guys. They don't give up till they're dead. And they're efficient and unemotional."

"I know."

"Three of them. That's like going up against a whole artillery division."

"You done?"

"We need a plan, Mason."

"I know," I said, grinning unpleasantly through my pain, "and we won't get one by sitting here talking about how wonderful they are."

"You stay here with Pamela. I go to the ladies'—"

"No. Why you?"

"Because, big guy, people expect ladies to take longer in the ladies' than men in the men's. So, while you two laugh and chat I kill the guy in the parking lot. I come back and join you."

My face told her I didn't like it, but I said, "Then what?"

She grinned. "This is the good bit. After coffee you get

in the Jag and stay close behind me. I take his car, go up the drive and smash it into the other team's vehicle. While they recover I jump in the Jag and we get the hell out of there."

I looked down at my hand and saw that it was swelling. The waitress returned with three plates of smoked salmon salad, told us to enjoy and went away again. I picked up the fork in my left hand and tried not to think about the throbbing pain in my right arm.

"That's a brilliant plan, Gallin. I only see one small flaw in it."

"What flaw?"

"The bit where you said, 'I kill the guy in the parking lot.' Don't get me wrong. You are very good at what you do, but you are a one-hundred-and-twenty-pound woman, and he is a two-hundred-and-twenty-pound slab of concrete out of one of the four most highly trained special forces regiments in the world."

She shrugged. "I killed his pal, didn't I?"

"After I broke his leg, yes."

"OK, so what do you suggest?"

I turned it around and looked at it from every angle. I stared at the black glass in the French windows and listened to the soft murmur of conversation, and the patter of rain. Finally I sighed. Gallin was halfway through her salad and Pamela hadn't touched hers. I said:

"You have to eat or you'll attract attention." While she picked up her fork and prodded her salad I said to Gallin: "I go out first and draw him away. Meanwhile you and Pamela run for the Jag."

"What about you? I'm a hundred-and-twenty-pound

girl, but you're a two-hundred-and-twenty-pound lummox with a broken hand."

"It's not broken, it's just—"

"Swollen and useless."

"OK, but I don't need my right hand to shoot him. I can shoot with both hands."

"Bullshit."

"It's not bullshit. I trained with both hands."

She sighed and shook her head. "Eat your salad. It's a crap plan and you know it."

"I am not letting you go out to face that man alone."

"Come on, Mason! I'm a trained soldier!" She dropped her voice to a hoarse whisper. "I'm Israeli special forces! You know that!"

I glanced around, aware we were getting intense. Nobody seemed to notice us. I spoke with quiet emphasis.

"These guys are very dangerous. They do not give up and they learn to ignore pain. I broke that guy's knee and he was still reaching for his gun to shoot me."

She grinned. "Who saved your bacon, Mason?"

I ignored her. "You cannot face him alone. He will kill you."

She became serious. "And he won't kill you, with a messed up right hand?"

"That doesn't matter. The important thing is that you can get Pamela to the airfield and continue the investigation. I'll take my chances."

I was surprised to see her face flush and her eyes become bright. She shook her head. "Wait, it's a little early for that kind of talk. We can work this out." She pointed at my plate. "Eat!"

We ate in silence and slowly the pain in my hand began to ease. The waitress came and took away our plates and replaced them with three rib-eye steaks. Pamela blanched and muttered, "I don't think I can."

Before Gallin could answer my phone pinged. I checked and said, "We have the location." I glanced at Gallin. She was cutting into her steak like she hadn't heard. She muttered, "OK. So put your phone away and eat your steak. What do we do?" She leaned back in her chair and waved to the waitress. "Bring us a bottle of house red, will you?" To me she smiled and said, "We're settling in for the evening, right? If they see us getting comfortable, maybe they'll even change their plans. Priority one is to get Pamela and at least one of us to the plane. But they don't know that. They just know we are here."

I nodded. "OK. So they think we are bedding down for the night, and they plan to come and get us at three AM in our rooms. Meanwhile we've gone."

"Right."

"So, how have we gone?"

"I'm working on that." She narrowed her eyes and wagged her finger at me across the table. Pamela had the look of a woman watching a terrifying tennis match. Gallin leaned forward. I put steak in my mouth and chewed. Gallin said, "When we go up to bed, they will go from red alert to orange or even yellow."

"Maybe."

"Shut up. They will have a time in their heads for the hit."

"Three AM."

"Not too early not too late."

"Right. So at two AM, one of us sneaks down and takes out Kiwi one."

"Have you brought a suppressor with you?" I sighed. "I didn't think so. So I take out Kiwi one, you come out and we leave. But here's another something."

I put more steak in my mouth and asked, "Anober shomshing?"

"When we come out of the hotel drive, instead of turning left we turn right and it leads us, in a roundabout way, to Biddeston and then Sheldon Airfield."

I swallowed and drained my glass. The pain was draining from my hand by the moment.

"It's good, Gallin. There is just one problem."

"What?"

"We have to be there in the next hour." She sagged back in her chair. Pamela asked her quietly, "Are we going to die?"

Gallin shook her head, not unkindly, and said, "Eat your steak. Drink your wine." She might have added, "It's probably the last you'll ever have," but she didn't.

I stood. Gallin scowled at me. "Where are you going?"

I leaned forward and spoke softly, "To the can. You want to come and hold my hand?"

"You'd better be back quick or I am going looking for you."

Pamela just said, "No…"

I made my way out to reception, but when I got there, instead of making for the toilets I headed out into the drizzle, holding my cell phone to my ear. I couldn't think of anything to say so I started rambling.

"No, his problem was not that he was transgender. His problem was that when he was a man he was a misogynistic bastard who was passionately anti-woke. But when he stopped taking the pills, Dave, he regressed into a violent, lesbian, woke activist..."

I was crunching slowly across the gravel, getting wet and talking like I meant it. I knew he could see me and was watching me, but I was pretty sure he couldn't hear me. I moved, apparently unconsciously, toward the parking lot.

"The question, Dave, is not whether you can can the cancan, but whether you can package the whole package and bottle the juice. You don't understand what the hell I am talking about? I'd be worried if you did, Dave. After all," I laughed, "you don't even *exist!* And I do *not* mean that in a pejorative sense."

There were 19th-century-style lamps placed around the lot. The light they cast glimmered on the tiny drops of drizzle as they fell, and in its dim glow I caught the lower part of a tweed jacket and a white shirt through the windshield of a Mercedes. I turned away, laughing ironically and gesturing with emphasis.

"No, Dave, it cannot wait until tomorrow! We need to move out *tonight!*" I paused, drawing closer to the Merc, watching my feet as they trod the drizzle. I knew he would not shoot me while I was on the phone for fear of setting up a general alarm. He would watch and wait, and try to listen. So I went on.

"I am very glad you are so confident. That is very reassuring. Oh, do I sound sarcastic? Maybe that's because I am being sarcastic! You are very confident that nobody knows where we are, but I am *not* that confident." I was maybe twelve feet away from his driver's door, and if he was listening, right now he would be confused, wondering what had happened to his pal and why I was not mentioning it to the fictitious Dave. I knew that what I had to do was keep talking with emphasis and keep his attention firmly on my words. So I raised my voice and got mad as I moved slightly beyond his door and into his blind spot.

"Yes! That's easy for you, Dave, goddammit! But you don't face getting murdered tonight. This guy does!"

As I said it I took a big step back, dropped my phone and wrenched open his door as I slipped the Fairbairn and Sykes from my boot. His expression was all about how mad he was at himself for all the things he hadn't done. He was fast. His right hand was already under his jacket, but the razor-sharp blade plunged deep into his left armpit, piercing his lung and his heart. He gasped and stared me in the eye. He didn't look scared, more mildly surprised, like he was thinking, *So this is how it happens?*

I pulled the blade out and the massive hemorrhaging made him sleepy. I finished it for him by slipping the blade down behind his left collarbone. He went into death quickly.

I closed the door quietly and wiped my prints off the handle, then walked quickly to the Jag. I fired up the engine and rolled to the entrance to the lawn, where the dining room was. There I called Gallin.

"You're calling me from the can? What is this, Mason? I thought respect was important to you."

"Step out onto the lawn. Bring Pamela. I'm waiting for you there in the Jag. I'll explain when you get here."

"You are one class A obstinate son of a bitch."

"You're welcome."

A moment later I saw them emerge in black stencils

from the warm glow of the French windows that led out from the dining room. Pamela was silent, but I could hear Gallin laughing and chatting like they were having a gas. But as soon as they were away from the windows they crossed the lawn at a half-run, and a moment later Pamela was climbing in the back and Gallin was getting in beside me and screwing a suppressor onto her Sig Sauer. I glanced at it as she closed the door and I pulled away.

"Where the hell did you have that?"

"You don't want to know. You OK to drive?"

I killed the lights and moved into the long tunnel of trees that shrouded the drive. "I'm OK. I drive, you shoot—if you have to. Pamela?" I glanced in the mirror and saw her terrified face looking at me through shadows. "Lie down on the floor, honey. And if anything happens to me and Gallin, get out and run like the hounds of hell are snapping at your ass. They will be."

She didn't answer, but she lay down out of sight.

I cruised slowly down the drive and stopped a few feet short of the gate. I didn't need to tell her. Gallin got out and moved silently to the shadows beside the exit and peered out both ways. Then she returned and climbed in. "You're good to go."

I pulled out, turned right and started driving north along a narrow road. I prayed to whatever gods look after spooks that we didn't meet anything coming the other way, because the road had room for one car and one car only. I kept the headlamps off and drove at a steady twenty miles an hour, and after about four minutes, up ahead I saw the lights of a farmhouse and beyond it I could just make out that the road turned sharp right.

That was when I looked in the mirror and saw two head-lamps moving up the road behind us. Gallin had seen it too.

"It could be a legit person using this lane."

I turned right and knew I was on a dead straight road almost a mile long. I hit the gas and accelerated to fifty miles an hour. I flipped on the lights, figuring we were far enough from the hotel, and if we weren't, we had already been seen. The lights in the mirror accelerated and started to close on us. After a couple of minutes I fishtailed into Hartham Lane. The Jag held the road and I avoided sideswiping a line of oaks by a couple of inches. I gunned the engine and moved up to sixty, speeding down a lane that was just wide enough for one car and had seven and eight-foot hedges either side.

In the mirror I watched the lights move into the road behind me. I eased my foot off the gas and said to Gallin, "They're not stupid enough to just try and follow."

"If they knew we were on this road, all they had to do was wait for us at the intersection up ahead."

"There's another car then, going to do just that. They're going to box us in. You'd better get down."

She slid down and I killed the lights again. I figured I was maybe three hundred yards from the intersection. I floored the pedal and in five seconds I was practically on the cross-roads. I could see a dark SUV up ahead, parked on the side-walk. Cursing Jaguar violently for removing the handbrake from their cars, I burst into the intersection. They opened up on us. I spun the wheel hard right, spinning into a donut, and shouted, "*Take 'em! Now!*"

# NINE

She didn't disappoint. Gripping the P226 in both hands, resting both forearms on the open window, she rained fire on the cab of the SUV as I did a donut in the middle of the intersection. And as I came around again, she emptied the magazine into them before I took off north and east along the A4 Bath Road, doing a hundred miles per hour. The SUV didn't follow.

Gallin rammed another magazine into the butt of the semi-automatic.

"How'd they know we'd left the hotel? How did they know we had turned right into the lane?" Suddenly I swore violently and started closing the windows. We had just passed the Bridgestone intersection. On the left we had dense woodland overgrown with ivy and ferns. I slammed on the brakes, spun the wheel and drove the Jag into the trees, sideswiping the heavy trunks violently and tearing down ivy as I went.

"*Get out!*" I bellowed. "*Get out! Get out! Get out now!*"

The car thudded to a halt, smashing the nearside head-lamp. Gallin had read my mind and was already out. She slammed her door and ran for the trees. I scrambled out, slammed my door and wrenched open the rear. Pamela was in the fetal position on the floor. I took a handful of her jacket and dragged her out, screaming at her, "*Run! Run! Run!*"

I hauled her in among the trees, pulled her down among the ferns and hissed in her ear, "*Don't breathe! Don't move!*"

Then I crawled on my belly back toward the Jag till I was just six feet from the trunk. I got to my feet and for a second stepped out where Gallin could see me. Then I dropped to my belly again.

I could hear the high whine of a speeding car approaching. It slowed as it reached the intersection and I saw a black Audi A4 pull up level with the Jag, with its hazards on, and two guys got out. The driver was tall and lean, with a crew cut and a brown leather jacket. His pal was shorter and stocker, with balding black hair and an Atilla the Hun moustache.

They approached the Jag, squinting at the windshield, trying to see inside the car. My heart was pounding and I was yelling silently at Gallin, "*Now! Now!*"

The driver pulled a suppressed semi-automatic from his belt and put two rounds through the driver's window. As he took a hold of the handle, the big moustache opened the back and peered in. There was the pop of compressed air and the crew cut's head spat brains all over the open back door and his pal's bald head.

I had sprung to my feet and started running when I had

heard the suppressed report. I scrambled around the trunk as the bald guy was wiping his driver's brains from his face. He stared at me and looked distressed as he said, "What...?" and reached under his left arm. I closed in, pinned his arm to his chest with my left hand and thrust at his belly with the fighting knife.

One of the cardinal rules in fighting is never to underestimate your opponent. This guy was a case in point. In his state of shock, caught by surprise, that blade should have gone home. Instead he weaved back, blocked me with his left arm and kicked me hard in the shin. And suddenly we had a problem. We had to finish it fast and get out of there, and now I was grappling with this son of a bitch.

I closed again, reached for the collar of his shirt, driving the knife hard at his belly. But his left hand caught my wrist and he smashed his right forearm into my elbow. The pain was excruciating and I almost dropped the knife. Next thing he was twisting my wrist out to put me in an arm lock.

I swore violently, jumped a foot in the air and came down hard with my elbow on his head. He staggered and let go of my wrist, but as I closed in to finish him he moved in and drove two good hooks into my belly, right and left. He winded me, and as I wheezed painfully I saw him grin and reach under his arm again. He was going to shoot me and there was nothing I could do about it because the pain in my chest was paralyzing me.

He pulled the Glock and held it to my head. I could see Gallin piling Pamela into the back of this bastard's Audi. I saw her turn and look, and the expression of horror as she saw what was about to happen. I saw his finger tighten on the trigger as Gallin turned, but it was much too late.

There was no human way she could cover the distance in the time.

He pulled the trigger and the gun exploded. I had already allowed my legs to fold and I felt the searing gases and the burning lead scorch my head as the slug skimmed a millimeter from my skull, and as my knees hit the grass I slammed the fighting knife into his belly. He fell back a step as Gallin collided with him and sent him crashing to the ground. She grabbed me and dragged me to my feet.

"Are you hurt? Are you OK? Speak to me! Are you OK?"

"I'm OK," I croaked, "but I think I'm deaf."

"Get in the passenger seat! Fast!"

She dragged me around the Audi, bundled me in the front passenger seat, vaulted the hood and slid behind the wheel. The tires squealed and it was the forward thrust of the car that slammed her door closed.

I wheezed painfully as we hurtled along the road. A quarter of a mile on we came to a fork in the road. She took the left fork without slowing and suddenly we were in a dark, country lane again. Dark fields flashed by beyond the black glass. I breathed slowly and deeply while shards of glass pierced my lungs. I felt sick and tried to ignore it.

Pamela said, "He's behind us."

Gallin snapped, "I know. Keep down."

I turned and saw the headlamps of my Jaguar gaining on us in the dark. They were unsteady and kept swerving, but they were gaining on us.

"I stabbed that son of a bitch in the belly," I said, half to myself.

"I told you. Those guys just don't give up."

We came to an intersection with practically zero visibility. She didn't slow. She leaned on the horn and hurtled across, fishtailed in and out of a bend and kept going without uttering a word. Two seconds later the headlamps behind us surged across the intersection, fishtailed and accelerated so his headlamps were flooding the cab.

Gallin shoved her gun in my hand and said, "Shoot the bastard!"

I somehow scrambled between the seat into the back of the car. Pamela was curled up in the corner, making noises like she was trying not to weep. Gallin swerved into another bend and I fell on Pamela. She screamed and I pulled myself into a kneeling position on the back seat. I was momentarily blinded by the massive glare of the headlamps. He must have been just ten or twelve feet behind us. I held the Sig in both hands, spread my knees wide and steadied my arms on the headrest.

That was when the rear windshield exploded. I covered my face with my arms, but the speed of the car and the slipstream carried the shattered glass away to spray the Jag behind us. I fired six rounds in rapid succession into the darkness above the glare of the headlamps. They swerved violently and for a moment I thought I'd hit him, but he kept coming.

Gallin yelled, "*Brace!*" and stood on the brakes. The tires screamed and I was hurled against the side of the car as the back end pivoted around the hood. Next thing the tortured engine was howling as we hurtled up a tree-lined drive and I struggled against the G-force to try and climb off Pamela. Up ahead, between the front seats, I could see the glow of the aerodrome. Against it I could see the silhouettes of the tower and the low, flat main building. In the black, plate-glass frontage our own headlamps were glaring, growing fast. Gallin yelled, "*Get ready to roll!*"

I glanced out the rear window. The Jag, momentarily delayed by the sharp bend, was gaining on us again. Pamela had started howling. I looked back and saw the glass front of the building hurtling at us. I screamed, "*Gallin! Stop!*" But it was too late. The Audi lurched onto the porch at a hundred and twenty miles per hour, left the ground and smashed through the plate-glass doors and window. We hit the floor, fishtailed and by the time the car had stopped Gallin already had the door open and was pouring lead into the windows at the rear of the building while I fell out of the back, grabbed a fistful of Pamela and ran after Gallin.

We stepped over the shattered glass out onto the tarmac. Through the drizzle I saw the Gulfstream, glowing among luminous needles of rain. The turbines whined and Gallin stood pointing at the jet, "*Go! Go! Go!*" I grabbed Pamela and dragged her toward the plane where I could now see the silhouette of the hostess in the doorway, staring at us. I shoved Pamela toward the steps and turned to look for Gallin.

She was on one knee, with her arms outstretched holding her Sig. I bellowed, "*Gallin! Come on! Now!*" and started running back toward her. Steady and deliberate she squeezed off seven rounds, then turned and started running toward me. I grabbed her, dragged her to the stairs and hurled her up. As I went up after her I looked back and saw a man staggering through the shattered window. He was holding a gun. I shoved Gallin and the stewardess in, bellowed, "*Go!*" at the pilot and started closing the door as the jet moved toward the runway.

Seconds later we were accelerating in a roar of engines. We lurched and suddenly we were being sucked up into the sky, banking west toward the North Atlantic and New York. I sank back in my leather seat and closed my eyes. I could hear Pamela sobbing, and Gallin telling the stewardess she needed a double Scotch and to get me one too.

Then I felt a jolt on my arm. I opened my eyes and managed to focus on her. She stared at me a moment and said, "What?" I frowned. She said, "You OK? Nurse is bringing you some medicine." I didn't say anything and she added, "I'm pumped."

"No kidding."

"You OK?"

"You already asked me that. I hurt. All of me. I think there may be a spot on my left heel that doesn't hurt."

"Yeah." She grinned. "You took some knocks today, huh?"

I shrugged with the shoulder that hurt less than the other. "Day's work."

She pointed at my hand. It was swollen and had started bleeding from under the sticking plaster. I said, "What?"

She pointed at it again and grinned. "Shooting a gun, knife fighting, with your hand like that? You're pretty badass under all that tuxedo shit." I closed my eyes and tried to repress the smile. "Drink your whisky, big guy. We're not done yet."

We landed in New Jersey's Teterboro airport at just after eleven PM. I had slept most of the way and had woken up just before touchdown with a bad headache and feeling vaguely nauseated. I checked my hand and found the swelling had gone down and it did not seem to be infected.

As we taxied toward the illuminated terminal, Pamela hurried to the toilet and Gallin reached over and put her hand on my arm.

"You good?"

I nodded and pointed through the window at four black limos that were speeding across the tarmac to meet us.

"That's either Nero, or the British government has issued a formal complaint against us."

"You think Sir John wants us back?"

I sat forward and heard myself creak. "What's not to want? Dead bodies strewn across the countryside, gunfights, wrecked cars, shattered airfields..."

"I know, right?"

Pamela emerged from the toilet looking a little less pale and sick. The plane had stopped, the turbines had run down and now the hostess opened the door for us onto the September night. She smiled sweetly as we descended the steps, like the last survivors of Armageddon, into the glow of the headlamps.

We were met at the bottom by four men in suits and long black coats. They identified themselves as ODIN and two of them took Pamela away to one of the limos. She looked fearfully over her shoulder at us and called back, "Where are they taking me?"

I gave her the thumbs up. "You'll be OK. We'll be in touch."

The other two led us to a second limo. We climbed in the back and found Nero seated, enveloped in a huge coat, staring at us. After a moment he settled his gaze on Gallin as the door closed with a soft thud.

"You father wanted me to inform you that Israel is not seeking a war with the United Kingdom."

"Thank you."

He turned to me. "And neither is the United States. You destroyed an airport."

I winced and thought about telling him it was Gallin's fault, but decided that would sound childish. Instead I said, "It seemed necessary at the time, sir. And the runway is still operational."

The look on his face told me "It was her fault" would have been a better choice. So I quickly asked, "Did you locate Barnes, sir?"

We pulled away and moved toward the airport exit. The lead car and the car carrying Pamela turned left and sped away. I figured they were headed for the I-95 and DC. We turned right, toward Manhattan.

"In a manner of speaking. He has a house on the beach at Stamford."

I frowned. "He has a *house?* In *Stamford?*"

His eyes became hooded and baleful. "People in Stamford have houses, Alex."

"Yeah, but why him? He just got here. He has always lived in London. An apartment, OK, but a *house?* In *Stamford?*"

"Perhaps you can ask him when you speak to him. But I warn you, he claims not to be home."

I stared at him a moment, then said a little sourly, "I guess that depends on who's calling."

He blinked slowly. "No doubt," he said. We both looked

at Gallin, who was softly snoring in the corner. "But before anything else you had better bathe and change your clothes. You appear to have a deal of blood on you. I trust it is not yours. Then we had better have a meal and discuss the chaos you seem to have stirred up."

I nodded at him and looked out the smoked window at the approaching lights of the Big Apple. "Sounds like a plan," I said.

# TEN

THEY DROVE US TO A LARGE BROWNSTONE ON West 89th Street. From the outside, by the light of the midnight streetlamps, it looked like two separate brownstones. But inside, it was all one. We rode an elegant, concertina elevator with lots of brass and mahogany, and little art deco lamps with green shades, up to the third floor, where I told Gallin good night, had a shower and fell into bed.

We slept like the dead for eight hours, and at nine in the morning I made my way down to the breakfast room where I found Gallin and Nero eating bacon, poached eggs, sausages, fried tomatoes, waffles, maple syrup, pancakes and fried bananas. There was also a pot of coffee, a jug of hot milk, another of double cream and three bowls of different colored sugar.

Nero grunted at me and waved me to a chair. "Sit. Eat. Captain Gallin has been telling me all about the beatings you received. You must be in need of protein. Focus on the protein and eschew the carbohydrates. The proteins will repair your damaged tissues."

He poured me a generous cup of strong coffee as I sat, and pushed it toward me repeating, with his mouth full, "Eat! Eat! The bacon is good." He gestured at Gallin while I helped myself to a bit of everything. "You, of course, are Jewish. You are forbidden pork. And this is my quarrel with religion. The advice of a wise man becomes the edict of a prophet, which in turn becomes the commandment of an unrelenting god. So the words that were uttered to guide people away from pain, become the instrument of condemnation against the infidel. Because the true sin in the Abrahamic religions, you understand, is disobedience. This they inherited from Mesopotamia, from the Anunaki of the Sumerians: you must obey the Mighty Ones, the Elohim. Plural, note."

I winced at him as I sipped my coffee. "This over breakfast?"

He ignored me and waved a piece of pancake in the air. "The Norsemen, indeed the northern tribes back into the Paleolithic age, would laugh at the notion of the gods dictating what you may and may not eat. It would be absurd, incomprehensible! But to the Sumerians, and those who followed them through Abraham and Sarah, this micromanagement was essential to control. Here was the birth of the hive-mind, part and parcel of the birth of modern, urban civilization. Put people in clay cells, separate them from the land, from the natural cycles of the Earth, tell them what to eat, what to drink, what to think, and above all, what *not* to think. Here is temporal power!"

I glanced at Gallin, expecting her to be studiously

ignoring him and focused on her food. Instead she was staring hard at him, silently absorbing every word he was saying.

He looked at me and gave a rare chuckle. "You!" he said, "You are a flippant, Anglo-Saxon playboy. You have no time for these worries, but I ask you, Alex, are we not living the same today? Are we not told daily what not to eat, what not to drink, what not to think and say? Each forbidden cigarette, each safety belt fastened, each crash helmet worn, each blasphemy law enacted, is a landmark on the road to Dystopia." He drained his cup and wagged a fat finger at me. "We charged them with building schools and roads, and defending the realm. Now they are telling us what not to say, what not to think and what not to feel. Believe me, we are in the suburbs of Dystopia already, and soon they will cull us. Soon, like the angry Elohim of the Old Testament, they will wipe us out!"

I sat looking at my eggs and bacon, sausages and waffles. Then I looked at him. "I thought you wanted me to eat."

"Forgive me," he said, like he didn't mean it. "I get carried away, and it is so rare that I have a beautiful woman to listen to me."

He gave her a smarmy smile. I glanced at Gallin and saw her blush. That made me feel unreasonably irritable.

"So, what's the plan with Barnes?" I said, and added a little venomously, "If you're done with the Elohim, that is."

I felt Gallin glare at me but ignored her. Nero took a big breath and said, "Well, clearly there is no point in phoning him, as that simply alerts him to our interest, and he does not want to be found."

I stuffed egg, bacon and bread into my mouth and spoke from behind my napkin as I wiped my lips.

"I think, given that Gallin is so captivatingly beautiful she distracts even the great minds of our time from their labors, we should use her as a bait to draw Barnes into a net."

"I'm right here, dork."

I feigned surprise. "Oh, sorry, I thought you were busy blushing. Do we know when Barnes starts back in the office? Or have we been too busy exploring the many names of Elohim to find out?"

Nero's eyes became hooded and he regarded me across the table. "Are you quite all right, Alex? Perhaps you should go back to bed and get up again."

"I'm fine. Barnes. Work. When?"

"He takes up his new position the Monday after next. We have made inquiries and he has a very small, select client base—a couple of major names in Hollywood, a couple of ex-presidents who have published autobiographies, and a couple of scandalous people who are now old and wise, and know the whereabouts of many skeletons. His specialization seems to be in the area of the ownership of information, with a healthy dose of offshore banking and trusts."

"Blackmail and dodging liability."

"That would be another way of putting it. We tried to make an appointment to see him but got the runaround."

Gallin stood. "That's bullshit. I'm just going to go and knock on his door."

"He won't be in," I told her.

She smiled at me. "He'll be in." Then she added, "I'll need to be wired. You wait outside. When I give you the word you come in."

When she'd gone Nero regarded me across the littered table and asked me, "Are you up to this?"

I scowled at him. "Of course I'm up to it. Why wouldn't I be?"

"You are unusually insolent and bad tempered. Something is clearly amiss."

"It's just my hand," I lied, and wondered why. "It still hurts a bit."

"Your hand..." The irony in his voice was so thick you could've spread it on toast. I showed him the hand, which was now very bruised but didn't hurt.

"I was bitten."

"I know you were bitten." He paused. "If you find, Alex, that the...*bite*...is affecting your ability to execute the job, kindly tell me, so that we can have a vet look at it for you."

I sighed. "I'm fine. I'll be OK."

"I say a vet because..."

"I get it! I'm behaving like an ass. I know. I'll be fine."

"Quite."

Half an hour later Gallin returned in a mauve satin dress with a slit up her left thigh that would have had the Nephilim fanning their blushing cheeks. "I need a car," she said. "Something a billionaire's daughter would drive."

A couple of phone calls to what Nero called the props department sourced her a 2021 Corvette in white with four hundred and ninety horsepower. "You need that just to knock on his door?"

"No, I need it so he'll open the door when I knock on it, and offer me coffee and the use of his telephone."

It was an hour's drive from West 89th Street to Nick Barnes' house on Wallacks Drive. The rain was as persistent here in New York as it had been in England, with huge, bellying clouds sailing in off the Atlantic, across Long Island and the Sound, trailing gray drapes of drizzle beneath them.

We took the Bronx River Parkway as far as the Bronx Park interchange and then turned east onto the Bronx and Pelham Parkway. At Pelham Bay Park we picked up the I-95 and settled into the flow moving north and east along the sound, through lush, green landscapes bedraggled by gray rain. We eventually took Glenbrook exit nine and came off onto Seaside Avenue, which we followed, by a tortuous path, to Willowbrook Avenue and finally to that other Eden, demi-paradise which was Wallacks Drive.

Wallacks Drive was all about maples and oaks and chestnuts, dry-stone walls and chimneypots peering through foliage. We cruised slowly down toward the beach until we came to a large gate that stood open, flanked by huge trees that might have been sycamores. It was hard to tell from the confines of the Corvette.

From the gate, a long, gravel drive bisected a perfect lawn to arrive at what might well have been a genuine Georgian mansion, with Greco-Roman columns supporting a Palladian pediment over a large porch with a shiny white door with a big, brass knob. Gallin parked across the gate, blocking all entry and exit, killed the engine and smiled at me. She put her hand over mine and said, "Don't be jealous, big guy. I am going to get soaked to the skin, but I'll be thinking of you."

"Take a hike." I said it with a reluctant smile and she winked and said, "Testing, testing." I switched on my earpiece. She repeated, "Can you hear me? My voice will be forever in your head."

"You're good."

Next thing she was out of the car, stamping her feet and putting on a show for the security cameras that must have been watching her. She kicked the wheel, then turned, looked at the impressive gates and went trotting down the drive toward the house.

I watched her banging on the door and ringing on the bell. I had to admit that to say she looked desirable would be the understatement of the century. It was hard to imagine how any red-blooded male could resist her.

The door opened and a man in a white jacket with white gloves peered out. I heard a wet crackle and, "My goodness!"

Then Gallin complaining, "My damn car broke down! Can I use your phone? Can you believe I left my phone at the restaurant? I really need to call my insurance company!"

"Of course, madam! Please come in!"

I watched her go inside and the door close. Then there was silence. I listened to the silence for ten seconds, thinking it sounded too absolute. I tapped the earpiece, switched it off and on again. There was nothing. I felt a stab of panic but suppressed it. There could be several reasons why the wire had stopped working, and most of them would be perfectly innocent. To go barging in now could compromise our whole operation. Gallin was extremely capable and it was far too soon to take action.

The was what my brain said. My gut was burning and telling me to get off my damned ass and do something. The result was that I shifted my ass six times in thirty seconds in my Corvette bucket seat and achieved nothing but an unsettled stomach. I somehow managed to hold on for five minutes and was about to climb out of the car when my phone jangled and made me jump.

I looked at the screen and saw it was Gallin.

"Yeah."

"Honey, Mr. Barnes has very kindly allowed me to use his telephone and made me a cup of hot chocolate. I told him you were waiting in the car and he insists you come inside."

"I'm on my way."

"Oh stop it, you old flatterer. Love you too!"

I climbed out of the car and was immediately soaked through. I hunched into my shoulders and trudged, feeling cold and wet and unreasonably sour, down the drive to the front door, where I hammered instead of ringing the bell. It was the kind of mood I was in. After a few seconds the same guy in the white coat and gloves opened the door. I smiled with a complete absence of humor. "I'm Honey..."

He blinked and smiled with an equal absence of humor. "How charming."

"I thought so. Mr. Barnes is expecting me."

He reached out. "Indeed. Allow me to take your coat." When he'd hung it up he led me across a spacious Georgian hall with a checkerboard floor to a set of tall, walnut doors. He paused and looked over his shoulder. "Whom should I say...?"

"Alex Mason."

He opened the doors, stood very erect and announced, "Mr. Alex Mason, sir."

I stepped into a large room with French windows overlooking a large lawn at the rear of the house. The décor was ostentatious, with a walk-in fireplace that was out of character with the house, overstuffed Victorian sofas and armchairs and what looked like genuine impressionists on the walls in heavy gilt frames. It tried to be eclectic but managed only to be pretentious.

Barnes was sitting on the sofa, close beside Gallin who was sitting in an armchair, holding a cup of steaming cocoa. She looked freshly toweled, with fluffy hair. They were both watching me. Barnes stood and moved toward me with his hand held out. He was tall, elegant and good-looking.

"Mr. Mason, may I offer you a hot drink? Please come and sit in front of the fire. Or perhaps you would like to go and dry off in the restroom first?"

I took his hand and we shook. "Thank you, Mr. Barnes. We won't keep you long. I have to be honest with you. After we phoned you in London and you gave us the appointment without telling us you were going to be in New York..."

He closed his eyes, then turned and smiled at Gallin. I went on:

"We thought maybe it would be best to drop in unexpected in case you decided to take up a post in Sydney." I sat. "I'm glad we caught you in."

"Aila Gallin, MI5. I *did* tell you I'd be traveling that afternoon, and you *did* miss our appointment." He sighed. "You want to talk to me about Saul. You have no jurisdiction here, you know?" He turned to me. "And you? Are you MI5 too?"

I tried not to look smug. I didn't try very hard. "I am attached to the Pentagon, Mr. Barnes, the Office of the Director of Intelligence. I have jurisdiction here."

He screwed up his face over a smile, like his own confusion amused him. "MI5, the Pentagon, the Director of Intelligence...? This is absurd! What in the name of God has Saul been up to?"

I stared at him a moment until he sat on the sofa and his smile faded. Then I told him, "We need you to give us his research, Mr. Barnes. Everything, including the completed manuscript for the show he was about to produce."

He stared back at me for a long moment. Then he took a deep breath. "I am sorry, Mr. Mason. In the first place, I am afraid I don't know what the hell you're talking about. In the second place I have been a lawyer far too long to allow myself to be intimidated by law enforcement bullyboy tactics. So, if you don't mind, I think I would like you to leave now. Get out, please!"

# ELEVEN

I looked at Gallin and smiled, and we both chuckled. I said, "You never practiced criminal law, Mr. Barnes, did you? It was always the high-end stuff for you. You see, you can do that to a cop, and he has to leave with his tail between his legs. You do that to us and we have several other options. We can shoot you in the knee and stick toothpicks under your nails,"

Gallin winced and added, "We don't often do that in leafy suburbs, though."

I nodded. "Or we can arrest you and take you to an undisclosed location for an indefinite period while we plant evidence linking you to a terrorist organization. Or we could take you up to the can and waterboard you in the bath. You see, we don't have jurisdiction as such. We are tasked with the security of the realm. We do whatever we have to do. Now, you tell me, Mr. Barnes, what do I have to do to get you to tell me where Saul's research and the manuscript are?"

He had gone very pale, and he looked very afraid, but his voice was firm when he spoke. "You can do whatever you see fit, but I can't tell you where it is because I simply don't know."

Gallin shook her head. "No, Nick. It won't wash. You were one of three people he was close to, in as much as Saul ever got close to anybody, plus you were his attorney."

"So what?"

She spread her hands. "So come on! He didn't give it to Pamela, his producer, he didn't give it to Julia, and it wasn't at his apartment..."

"So you thought you'd come and terrorize one of the innocent citizens you are tasked with protecting, by threatening him with murder and torture."

"Where is it, Nick?"

"I have no idea. I had largely lost touch with Saul. He had always been arrogant and conceited, but in recent years he had become insufferable. And we were never really friends anyway. Saul had no friends. The closest thing he had to a friend was his Julia. I had grown bored with him and we had largely lost touch." He paused and after a moment, as an afterthought, he said, "Maybe you should be talking to his bit of fluff, Naomi Gordon, instead of me."

Gallin laughed. "Come on, Nick! You knew Saul! He would not have entrusted his work—especially work he considered so important—to a girlfriend. You know that. There is only one person he would have entrusted it to, and that is you."

He spread his hands. "Well, I'm sorry. However logical you may think that sounds, he did not entrust it to me. And if he had..."

He trailed off and shook his head. I said, "If he had, what?"

"Nothing. Forget it."

"It would have been a coup, right? Saul was an international celebrity. And if this documentary was as sensational as he was claiming, that would make him an A-list client. You were going to say that if he had entrusted it to you, you would not have left London, at least not just then."

I waited. He didn't say anything. I went on.

"But maybe that was precisely why you did leave."

"It had nothing to do with it one way or the other."

"When was the last time you saw Saul?"

He hesitated. "I don't recall exactly. Two or three weeks ago."

"What was the occasion?"

"Um..." He shook his head at the floor. "I don't recall. He telephoned me did I want to have a drink? Something like that."

"He wanted to talk to you."

"Um, I suppose..."

"What did he talk to you about?"

He was getting nervous. "Look, I honestly don't remember. I think he was talking about ditching Naomi—"

"Did he want to try again with his wife? Was that it?"

"It may have been. We just had a quick drink and that was it."

"There was something else he talked to you about?"

"What do you mean?"

"He told you his documentary was going to rock the world. He wouldn't have been Saul if he hadn't."

"Oh, well, yes."

I laughed like suddenly we were friends laughing about a mutual acquaintance. "I mean, you'd known each other for years. You had been his lawyer for a long time and one of your areas of expertise was Intellectual Property. It was natural he would tell you about the project and what a knockout it was going to be."

He saw too late he had walked into a trap and sighed.

"All right, Mr. Mason, yes. He called me because he wanted to talk about the implications of the documentary, and asked me to read it and give him and Pamela an assessment of the risks involved—libel, defamation, slander..."

"And?"

He raised his eyebrows high and gave his head lots of little shakes, like he was getting tired of telling us the same thing over and over.

"I said no. I told you, I wanted nothing more to do with him. And besides, I thought he had gone a bridge too far. These were not mid-range senators, mayors and industrialists he was going after. These were multinational corporations within the so-called military-industrial complex. These people are above the law. They are very powerful and very, very dangerous. I didn't want anything to do with it."

"Did he tell you what it was about?"

"Only in very general terms. And I didn't really want to know. I'd rather not be written off as a suicide after being thrown from the sixteenth floor of a skyscraper, thanks very much."

We were silent for a moment before I observed, "You took him seriously, then."

He didn't answer straight away. He looked at his left palm and rubbed it with his thumb. Finally he said, "Yes, I took him seriously. It was always a mistake not to take Saul seriously. That was the last time I saw him."

I grunted. "I am going to ask you to make a guess, Mr. Barnes. If you haven't got it, and neither Julia nor Pamela has it, where is it? Where do you think it is?"

"I don't know," he said to his palm, and then looked up at me. "And I don't want to know. They killed Saul for digging into matters that were out of bounds. And they will kill anyone else who tries to do the same. Please, don't get me involved."

I gave a small laugh. "Not twenty minutes ago you were screwing your face up, all confused, and you said, and I quote, 'MI5? The Pentagon? The Director of Intelligence...? This is absurd! What in the name of God has Saul been up to?' Now you are telling me he was going up against the might of the military-industrial complex. You're telling me he called you to discuss this with you. That you went to meet him, but that you told him you didn't want to know? I don't believe you, Mr. Barnes. I think you're lying."

Gallin spoke up, laughing and shaking her head. "What Mr. Mason means, Nick, is that you are so full of bullshit you could fertilize Kansas. And if you seriously think we are just going to shrug our shoulders and walk away, you must be out of your tiny mind. You're involved, Nick. It's too late. Now you have to choose: you help us, or you help them."

He stared at her for a moment, then said, "I'm sorry. I don't know any more than I have told you."

I sighed heavily and stood. "You know one thing."

He frowned at me. "What?"

"You know what companies he was investigating. He told you and you have admitted as much by saying they were part of the military-industrial complex. Who are they, Mr. Barnes?"

He had gone a waxy gray color. He was terrified. He swallowed hard a couple of times, then shook his head. "No, I'm sorry. He didn't say anything about that. You know who the military-industrial complex are. You work for them! But he did not mention any names. You are mistaken about that."

"Yeah?" I handed him my card. "So how come it's got you so scared if he didn't tell you anything about it? You seem to me to know a lot for somebody who doesn't know anything. If you change your mind, call me." I paused. "And, Nick? You'd be wise to change your mind."


A couple of hours later we were sitting in Patsy's Pizzeria. It was dark outside and a handful of wet, colored lights stained the black glass of the restaurant window. Indistinct figures moved past, all hunched, bent against the incessant rain. We had a couple of beers sitting on the table. The TV was murmuring in the background. There were two guys sitting up at the bar. We'd ordered a couple of pepperoni pizzas, and I could smell them being made. My stomach said that was a good thing. My brain was lost in a dark place, and as I watched the dark figures process past the black glass, through the moist lights in the wet world outside, my dark unconscious mind kept repeating a phrase, over and again... Then Gallin said it, suddenly, for no particular reason: "The military-industrial complex."

I nodded. "Eisenhower warned against it, and he wasn't

wrong. In mundane, temporal terms, it now has absolute power."

"But," she wagged a finger at me, "for that to be true, for that power to be exercised, there would have to be some kind of unified, administrative body, and a president—something or somebody to *focus* that power on an objective. It's like, you have ten, fifteen regiments, but no general HQ to coordinate them. Before long what you have is chaos and anarchy. There has to be a central point of focus."

I nodded and let my gaze drift back again to the black glass and the splashes of colored light.

"That is a frightening thought."

"Yeah, especially when you consider the amount of black money which is channeled secretly every year into so-called 'black projects.' What is it at the last estimate?"

I took a deep breath. "The fiscal year 2021, the budget appropriation *included*, but was not limited to, just shy of sixty-one billion for the National Intelligence Program, and a little over twenty-three billion for the Military Intelligence Program. This year it was a little over sixty-two billion for National Intelligence, and a shade over twenty-three billion for Military Intelligence. And then there is the money that simply disappears, which nobody is accountable for. Some put that up in the trillions of dollars. The fact is that classified accounts, red tape and deliberately sloppy accounting means it is impossible to know how much gets siphoned off for even blacker budgets and research."

She studied her beer. "All of which underscores the fact that they, whoever they are, are unaccountable. They answer to nobody."

"Nero once told me that violence is the single most valuable commodity on the planet. He said it was the only true source of power. He who can inflict most pain, wields the most power. That is a fact that the military-industrial complex understands fully. Whatever the Constitution says, whatever Congress may say, the raw truth is that the federal government lives in an uneasy truce with those who wield the real power." I stared at her for a long moment before adding, "And I guess Barnes is right. I am an instrument of that power."

She looked up from her glass, startled, then said, "ODIN."

"It is the ultimate expression of that power. It doesn't exist officially, so it is not accountable to anyone, yet it has access to virtually inexhaustible funds, and can project its power—violence—to any part of the globe. We are intimately enmeshed with the military-industrial complex that Eisenhower feared so much. We are a part of it, and we are here to protect it."

She didn't say anything for a moment. Her gaze shifted out to the same dark, wet street I'd been watching. After a while she said, "What about you?" And then, "What about Nero? I mean as people..."

I frowned at her. The waitress brought over our pizzas and I asked her for a couple more beers. When she went away again I said:

"There are things I don't understand. I mean, for a start, why the hell have we been asked to investigate this? If we are talking about a renowned journalist being assassinated as part of a conspiracy, by a coordinated, organized...," I searched the walls of the restaurant for the right word, "*administration* that actually runs the military-industrial complex, that has to all intents and purposes become a deep state in its own right—"

"And we are," she interrupted. "That is precisely what we are talking about."

I nodded. "Then by sheer force of logic, irresistibly, we have to conclude that ODIN is an integral, fundamental part of that system."

"I can't see how we can avoid that conclusion."

"So the next step we have to take is to conclude that Nero, as the director of ODIN, knows about this and is a party to it." She nodded and I went on. "So if he—Nero—knows that the military-industrial complex has effectively developed into an organization in its own right, with its own management and internal governing structure, if he knows that and knows that ODIN is part of that structure, why has he tasked us with investigating Saul's death and exposing this conspiracy?"

Gallin scowled at me, like she was really mad at my question, and watched me tear off a chunk of my pizza. When I'd bitten into it and started chewing she held up two fingers in the "V" sign.

"Two reasons: one, so that when he shuts the investigation down he can legitimately claim he put his best agent on it *and* called in outside help; two, he didn't, it was Sir John who started this investigation."

I squinted and swallowed. "What are we saying, that Sir John is on the side of the angels and wants to expose Frankenstein's monster?"

She shrugged. "I don't know. Frankenstein's monster was created by the US in the shape of President Truman. Maybe—and I am just speculating here—maybe the other

Five Eyes nations, or Sir John, are not comfortable with what the American state is becoming." She paused and screwed up her face. "I mean, we are talking about a non-democratic, immensely powerful deep state existing *inside* the United States. I think a lot of foreign countries must be nervous about that. Britain is the States' closest ally—Brutus to America's Caesar. Hell! It is even possible that people within Congress or the White House have asked ODIN to intercede as a multinational organization."

"I don't buy Nero knowingly being a party to something like this."

"How well do you know him? How well does anybody know Nero? The man wields a lot of power. Presidents shut up and listen when he talks. He's a dark horse, Alex."

I looked down at my pizza and suddenly had no appetite. "So if this is right, our task was not to find who killed Saul, but to find his missing work."

She raised her eyebrows and nodded. "Yeah, that makes sense. I think that's right."

"And if and when we find it, we will tacitly be offered a choice: toe the line and bury the research, or join Saul on a six-foot holiday."

"That may be an extrapolation too far."

I shook my head. "I don't see why. It is the next logical step. If Saul was a threat, so would we be if we found and read his research."

She picked up a piece of pizza and dropped it suddenly and angrily on her plate.

"Shit, Mason! Where did this suddenly come from?"

I didn't look at her. My eyes were fixed on the darkness outside, and the incessant rain. "It came from Saul's lawyer, and his closest ally. I don't buy that he would suddenly, after all these years, drop his best client because he was getting on his nerves." I glanced at her. "I'll tell you something else. I keep thinking of the way Pamela was taken away when we arrived. I can't shake the feeling that this is an unholy mess. I think we have strolled carelessly into one mother of a mess, Gallin. We have drifted up Shit Creek, and we have no paddle."

# TWELVE

GALLIN WAS INSIDE. I COULD SEE HER THROUGH the glass in the window, hunched over her beer. I was standing in the porch and I turned to watch the traffic hissing slowly over the blacktop. Breaking the wet runnels of light. There were not many people out and the few there were, were bent under their umbrellas, hurrying home.

Nero answered on the second ring. He sounded tired.

"Alex, I have told you not to—"

"Shut up, sir." He went quiet, didn't answer, and then I knew we were in real trouble. "We are going back to London tonight. But before we go we need to talk."

"Yes," was all he said. "Yes."

"When?"

"Can you come now?"

"Where?"

"89th Street."

"I don't trust it."

"It will be secure. For now, at least. Anywhere else..." He sighed heavily. "Anywhere else will be more risky."

"We'll be there in twenty minutes."

I hung up and pushed inside. Gallin looked up and watched me approach. Her eyes searched my face. If my face told her anything it told her I felt sick. "Let's go."

"Where?"

"89th Street."

"That's not smart, Mason."

"Yeah, that's what I told him." I went to the bar and paid the bill. When I got back to the table Gallin was still sitting, watching me like she was waiting for something. I said, "He told me it had to be there. We haven't the time to argue. Nero is not bent. I'll stake my life on it. If he says 89th Street is OK for now, I believe him."

I was going to tell her if she wanted to wait in the car she could do that. But I knew that wasn't what she was saying. She sighed and stood, but when we got to the car she said, "You wait in the car. I'll go up."

"Why?"

"Because I am not ODIN. I'm Mossad. They might balk at taking me out. You're ODIN. You'll be a legitimate target for them."

I walked round the car and stood close to her. "Thanks, but I don't think they're squeamish. We're in this together. Where you go, I go."

She thumped me gently on the chest with her fist and got in behind the wheel. I went back to the passenger side and climbed in beside her. We drove at a sedate pace through the dark rain. We didn't speak. The hiss of passing cars and the squeak and thud of the windshield wipers were the only sounds among the haze of passing headlamps.

We eventually crossed the black water into Manhattan, and pretty soon we were cruising down Central Park West and turning in at 89th Street. We parked outside and I got out and looked up at the dark mass of the building. All the windows were black, but on the fourth floor there was a dim glow in the corner window.

Gallin got out and stood beside me. "It's wrong," she said softly. I could feel the small droplets of water accumulating on my scalp. A trickle ran down my forehead. A crazy voice in my head told me I could feel that because I was alive.

I moved up the stairs. The door buzzed as I approached it and I pushed it open onto a pitch-dark hall. I pulled the Sig from under my arm and moved in with Gallin aiming her weapon over my shoulder. We let the door close behind us and spread out into the dark hall. We hunkered down into the corner and listened. There was absolute silence.

I pulled the pencil flashlight from my jacket and shone it on the stairs. Gallin moved forward and shone her torch up the stairwell. I moved in after her and climbed to the first landing. In that way we moved to the top floor and Nero's office. The darkness—and his silence—were unnerving.

We shared an unspoken awareness that we were neglecting the rooms on each floor we left behind, but we were also aware of a sense of urgency, and to check each room on each floor would have been logistically almost impossible. So instead, whoever was behind checked the rearguard and we moved as fast as we could to the fourth floor, and then along the dark passage toward where limpid light filtered from under the closed door of the corner office.

We stood either side of the door. My belly was on fire and I could feel my heart pounding hard in my chest. I knew I was going to kick in the door and find him sitting behind his desk with a napkin tucked in his collar, a bottle of Pol Roger beside him and a whole lobster in front of him. He'd arch an eyebrow at me and make some sarcastic crack.

I reached across, turned the handle and eased the door open as we both stood back. Nothing happened. I hunkered down and peered around the door. There was one lamp burning. It was on his desk and cast a pool of dark amber. In its circle I could see Nero's hands. I recognized them because they were large and fat, and he had a signet ring on his left baby finger. I could see his white, starched cuffs and I could see his large belly and his charcoal, pinstriped vest.

I moved in, aware of Gallin behind me, scanning the corners. I moved to the desk and shone my flashlight on his face. He was looking back at me with one steady, unblinking eye. I tried to speak. I tried to say, "Sir?" but my mouth was pasty and dry, and my breathing had become tight. And it would have been pointless to speak to him anyway. Because dead men don't talk.

His eye was wide and steady, and his face was impassive. It showed no sign of fear, in spite of the gaping, black and red cavity which had replaced his left eye. There is a time and a place for emotion, and this was not it. I knew I had to file my feelings away for later. But I knew also I would mourn this most remarkable giant. In time I would mourn him, and I would miss him.

Gallin stood beside me.

"It's a joke," I said, and my voice was a rasp.

"*What?*" She looked at me like I was crazy.

"Old One Eye," I said. "Odin was known as Old One Eye. He lost his eye in his search for ultimate knowledge. This is their idea of a joke."

And in silence I made him a solemn promise, that I would find them, I would kill them and I would bring their tower burning to the ground.

Gallin said, "So who buzzed us in?"

We ran, silently, taking the steps three and four at a time, working systematically, keeping each other's backs, moving from room to room, praying the killer was still there. But when we came to the kitchen in the basement we found the back door open, and not a trace of the killer to be found. He had let us in because he wanted us to find Nero, but he had left like a ghost while we were climbing the stairs.

I sat on the kitchen doorstep, with occasional spatters of rain hitting my face, and called ODIN in DC. I was not put through voice recognition. Lovelock answered straight away. She said, "You picked a fine time."

I bit back the lump in my throat and said, "You know I'd never leave you, Lucille."

"Not with four hungry children?"

"Not with a crop in the field."

"Where is he, Alex? I am worried sick. He hasn't checked in for hours!"

"He's dead, Lovelock."

"Oh, no..." She said it like I'd told her the pie had burned in the oven. And then repeated it with grief creeping into her voice, "Oh, *no*..."

"Did he leave you any message, did he say anything?"

She thought for a moment. "He said he was going to be

away for a few days, to keep things going if he went off the radar."

"When did he last contact you?"

"This morning. Alex, what happened?"

"I spoke to him less than an hour ago. Lovelock, let's keep this short. Now listen to me very carefully, OK?"

"OK—"

"Nero is alive and well. I'm telling you I have just seen him. He'll be in touch soon. You keep things running in his absence, just like he said. You follow his orders, OK? You understand me?"

"Yes, Alex." She said it with infinite sadness. "I understand."

"I'll be in touch."

"Yes."

"Are we good, Lovelock?"

"We're good."

I looked at Gallin. "We need to go. Call the pilot. Tell him we're on our way. We need to get back to London. Now."

We made our way out through the basement. While she dialed she said, "London, why? Talk to me."

"We need to talk to Sir John. But I want to show up unexpectedly."

She cut me short and started talking into the phone. "Hey, Captain Gallin. We need immediate relocation to Madrid. We're on our way to Teterboro now... Yeah, Madrid, Spain."

We loped through the rain to the car and climbed in. As we slammed the doors I said, "Madrid?"

She fired the engine and we pulled away, moving west

and then north toward the George Washington Bridge. She glanced at me.

"I'm being careful, Mason. We don't know who our friends are or who our enemies are. I trust you because I am a sentimental fool."

"I'm touched."

"Don't be stupid. It's the same reason you trust me. We just don't know, Mason. That pilot could be on the phone right now to ODIN brass telling them we are headed for Madrid and to be ready for us."

"Agreed." We were quiet for a while, moving north up Amsterdam Avenue. Then I repeated, with more emphasis, "Agreed, and we have a problem so big, I have no idea, Gallin, how we are going to solve it. We don't know who in ODIN, or who in the federal government, is out to get us. You can withdraw to Mossad and they will protect you. But if the Pentagon decides to come after me..." I trailed off.

After a moment she shook her head. "Nah," she said. "Things can't get that crazy, Mason. Somewhere the madness has to stop."

We looked at each other, and I watched as the lights and shadows of the avenue washed slowly across her face. After a moment she looked back at the road and said, "It has to stop, right?"

I looked away. I couldn't answer. The only man I knew who might have been able to answer a question like that was dead. Nobody had ever got close enough to Nero to be his friend, or to claim to love or be loved by him. But over the years he had become... I faltered in my own thoughts. Had become what? Somebody I trusted, somebody I turned to when I needed guidance, somebody I knew would go the extra mile. More than a mentor, more than a guide, more than a friend.

And I was having real trouble assimilating the fact that he was dead, and I could no longer turn to him for guidance or help.

I was on my own. I turned to Gallin again as we moved slowly past the Trinity Church Cemetery.

"We're alone," I said, unsure if it was hope or despair I could hear in my voice. Then added, "I'm alone."

She scowled. A little later we turned onto the George Washington Bridge. The traffic was light and she accelerated through the rain. She didn't say anything, but you could feel the aggression in her movements, and in the growing, urgent speed of the car.

She came off the I-95 at exit 66 and we wound through empty, suburban wastelands in South Hackensack until we came to Industrial Avenue. There she turned right and left and next thing we were pulling into the airport. All the way she said nothing. She parked, we climbed out of the car and she came around the trunk toward me. There she thumped me hard in the chest with the heel of her hand and, as I backed up a step she pushed me so I stumbled against the wall. There she punched me hard in the chest, so I raised my voice and snapped, "Hey! Cut it out!"

"*You're alone, you son of a bitch?*" She thumped me in the chest again. "*I should slap your face, you ungrateful bastard!*" She thumped me again, with both hands on my shoulders. "*You're alone?*" This time she didn't hold back and slapped me hard across the face with her open palm.

"*Gallin! Stop it, for Christ's sake!*"

"*You're alone?*" She slapped me again with her left hand

and raised her voice. "*You're alone? You son of a bitch! So tell me this! Who's slapping your big, ugly ungrateful face!*"

She swung at me again but I caught her wrist.

"Stop it."

She wrenched her hand free. "Let go of me!"

She turned and marched toward the airport building where we were to meet the pilot. I called after her but she ignored me and kept going through the rain. I followed and when I got inside I saw her talking to the pilot over by the check-in desk. He greeted me and fifteen minutes later we were settled in the plane and the hostess was closing the door, ready for takeoff.

As we taxied toward the runway I said, "Gallin?" She didn't answer, so I said, "Captain?"

She turned and looked at me with eyes that were not friendly or inviting. "What?"

"What I said was unintentionally callous and insensitive. Please forgive me if I appeared ungrateful. I am anything but. I don't know what I would do, or where I would be, if I did not have you to slap me around and beat me up." There was no hint of a smile, but I pressed on. "Nero's death has hit me harder that I could have expected." Her gaze shifted away from my face. "I didn't realize how fond I was of the old guy, or how much I had come to depend on him. I will confess to you that I am kind of rudderless right now. I am not just worried, I am scared. For me, but especially for you."

A flash of anger and challenge in her eyes. "You don't need to be scared about me!"

"I don't need to, no. But let me ask you something,

Gallin. Are you scared for me? Are you worried about what might happen to me?"

She scowled again and looked away. "You know I am, you son of a bitch!"

"Yeah, well it cuts both ways. I don't need to be scared for you, but I am anyway. Because I care about you. Probably too much. I know I am never alone as long as I have you. I know that and believe me, I am grateful. And you know you'll never be alone as long as you've got me."

"Oh, great! That's just great!" She looked away at the window. The engines roared and whined and the jet began to accelerate down the runway. Just before she was drowned out by the roar of the engines she said, "Now I can't even be mad at you!"

We leapt into the sky and soared out over the black Atlantic as the tiny lights fell away below us. After a while she undid her belt and slipped across the aisle into the seat beside me. There she took my arm in both of hers, rested her head against my shoulder and began to snore softly.

# THIRTEEN

FOR THE NEXT HOUR I SAT AND STARED AT THE blackness outside the small, oval window. The same thoughts kept marching by my mind's eye in a mocking procession, like they knew something I didn't know. When Saul's killer turned up, Saul no longer had his work in his apartment—that much had become obvious partly from logical deduction, but also because Simon the janitor had told us so. *So the person who'd turned up to kill him was not after his work.*

They were after Saul.

It was also obvious that whoever had killed him was on close terms with Saul—as close as anybody ever got—and that narrowed the field to his ex-wife, his lover, his producer and his ex-lawyer. None of whom struck me as remotely likely.

For a start, the killer had been cool and clinical to a point you would expect from a sociopathic professional. He had shot Saul in the face at point-blank range and his hand had not wavered. That Julia Epstein, his ex-wife, could have done that defied credulity to the point of absurdity. And trying to visualize Naomi Gordon doing that was too fantastic to contemplate. That left Pamela and Nick Barnes.

Remembering the state Pamela was in when we collected her from her cottage in Cornwall was enough to convince me she could not have done it. Besides which, she had no motive. He was about to make her very, very rich, and an eminence in her profession.

Which left Nick Barnes.

There was no doubt he was smooth, and you do not rise to his heights in the legal profession without having a certain amount of cold blood in your veins. Could I see him putting a gun in his friend's face and pulling the trigger from just a few feet away, while looking him in the eye?

First I concluded I didn't know. Then I concluded maybe it would depend on how motivated he was. After that I decided I had absolutely no grounds for reaching that conclusion.

Then Gallin stirred, took a deep breath and looked at her watch. She rose from her seat and walked, slightly unsteady to the cockpit, where she knocked and opened the door, while pulling the Sig from under her arm. There was a short squeal from the hostess. And then Gallin said quietly, "Oh, don't worry about this, I was just going to clean it. Captain? You need to change course for London Stanstead. You'll advise the tower of the change of plan, but if you advise anybody else I will shoot you and your cute stewardess and throw you both into the Atlantic. It's nothing personal, just orders from the Pentagon, you understand?"

The pilot was cool. He stayed calm and said, "London Stanstead."

"Correct. When we get there you go on your way, nothing happened. You cause problems, advise anybody of the change of plan, and then we start getting problems. Not worth it."

"I understand."

"That's ma'boy." She turned to the stewardess. "How about something to eat, sweet cheeks?"

She came back and sat opposite me across the table. I said, "Are you psychotic?"

"Nah." She shook her head. "I pretend because it makes people more cooperative if they think you're psychotic. But actually I am perfectly sane." She smiled. "What were you thinking while I was sleeping?"

I gave her a rundown and concluded, "The only person I can remotely imagine killing him is Barnes, but it seems pretty unlikely. Which means two things: either I have completely misread Barnes and he is a sociopath, or there is somebody else Saul was close to, that we don't know about."

She took a deep breath, fell back in her chair and puffed out her cheeks. "You know what I think? I think we have come to the end of this path, and we have everything we are going to find down here. We need to go and explore a completely different avenue."

I held up my fingers in the V-sign. "Two. Two avenues."

"Right, two avenues. One is FUCCIT. We need to find out who the CEO is and take him, along with the whole board of directors, to the Sahara, cover him in honey and feed him to the ants until he tells us what the hell is going on. And two...?"

"Two is we need to talk to Sir John again and throw a scare into him. I want to know who killed Nero. And when I find out, I am going for them."

She was shaking her head. "You can't make this personal."

"It is personal. You know it's personal. We are way past doing a job, Gallin. We don't even know if we have an employer anymore. We don't know if the damned Pentagon has gone rogue. Hell, we could be in the middle of a coup d'état in DC. The only way this makes any sense at all, is if it's personal."

She gave the kind of sigh that said she agreed with me, though her common sense said she was wrong.

"He was one of a kind," I added. "He was the kind of man the world needs, an original, humane, committed to protecting what he believed in. The world will be an uglier place now he's gone. I have to avenge him."

"We have to avenge him. I'm pretty sure my father will help. Nero was a friend to Israel. We don't forget our friends."

I gave her a grin you could call rueful. "No kidding."

———

It was nine AM by the time we touched down in Stanstead airport. As we were leaving the plane Gallin stopped and stood close to the pilot and the stewardess. She looked serious, almost sad. "It's a mess," she said. "It was never meant to be like this. We thought we were fighting for freedom. Now it's bigger than any of us. People like us don't exist. We are shadows. Don't get involved. It's not your fight. Best you just forget. Forget."

We crossed the main hall and went out toward the large parking lot. There was no rain but the sky was heavy with gunmetal clouds, and there was a chill in the air that crept in under your collar and made you shudder. As she pulled her cell from her pocket she said, "You try to read their thoughts. You have to go kind of passive and receptive and try to pick up what they are thinking. Then you put it into words for them. It can have a deeply hypnotic effect. Hi, Dave? Listen—"

She turned away from me, talking into her phone in Hebrew. She strolled up and down for a bit, with her left hand in her pocket, looking down at her feet. She was silent for a while, then I heard her say, "Ah-bah, ah-bah," a couple of times and after that she started talking again. Finally she said, "Love you too, Daddy," and hung up.

She came back to me and I said, "What?"

"We have a place for a couple of weeks in Acton, and we can pick up a rental from Avis in about fifteen minutes."

"OK, good, so the first thing we need to do is get whatever information we can on FUCCIT and their CEO. You could do that while I go and have a chat with Sir John."

I made to move toward the airport building again but she stayed put, chewing her lip and looking up at the sky. "What's the plan?" she asked.

"What?"

"What's the plan, Mason? How do we normally operate? We execute orders and we provide intelligence. So what are we doing now? When we get the intel on FUCCIT, what do we do with it? Who do we give it to? And once the intel is delivered, whose orders are we going to execute? Or are you just going to find a way to get close to the CEO of FUCCIT and shoot him?"

I didn't answer. I couldn't. She went on, "You know as well as I do that as soon as I start looking into this corporation, I am going to find it is connected one way or another to a whole string of other companies and corporations that all feed back to the big five, and through them to a couple of desks at the Pentagon. So what's our plan?"

The cold damp breeze crept down my neck and my back. I shuddered. A wave of depression washed over me and I fought to shake it off.

"The plan," I said, "provisionally, is collect the car, go to the apartment, make lots of coffee, have brunch and make a plan. Is that good enough for now?"

She nodded. "That'll do for now."

———

THE CAR TURNED out to be a Skoda Octavia. The only Octavia I could think of was the one who married Mark Antony and raised the kids he had with Cleopatra like they were her own. That made the name of the car more interesting than the car itself, which was not remarkable in any way.

It got us to Acton, by way of the M11 freeway, the A406 and a shopping mall where we bought essentials including food and clothes. After that we wound through leafy neighborhoods that probably looked great on a sunny day in spring, but that morning looked like depression made suburb.

East Acton wasn't much better. It was a cluster of quiet, leafy roads that should have been cute but were all infected by the vast, industrial ugliness of the A40 road that cut through southern England like an infected gash from an avenging sword. The "place" Gallin's father had arranged for us turned out to be a large, 1930s house with a paved front yard for the car and a big backyard with a lawn and a giant sycamore tree. A dirt path led up the side of the house to a back gate.

Opposite the house was the King Fahad Academy, minaret and all. We parked Octavia, and Gallin climbed out into the mid-morning drizzle. She jerked her head at the school across the road.

"This is my father's sense of humor. He says he liked to keep an eye on it from time to time. 'This is where they teach girls to be ashamed of their hair and their faces,' he says, 'and boys to be ashamed of their humanity.'"

A voice at the gate made me turn. It was an old guy with an Australian hat and a bike which he was wheeling.

"They told me there was a B&Q, or a Texas Home Stores..."

Gallin approached him smiling. "That was a long time ago, when there were still Hobbits in the hedgerows."

"That long ago?" He laughed. "Well, I'd better continue my quest. Shake."

He held out his hand and they shook, and he went off with his bike, lurching down the hill. I said, "Hobbits in the hedgerows? Seriously?"

She shrugged. "My father believes Tolkien had a lot to teach us. His books contain many keys." She held up the key the old guy had slipped her and moved toward the door.

Inside, the house was dark and smelled of stale tobacco. On the left, two doors led to a front room with a bow window that was furnished as an office, and a living room at the back with French windows onto the lawn. Beyond that was a large kitchen-diner, and a flight of stairs on the right led up to the bedrooms and a bathroom.

We unloaded the trunk of the car and Gallin made a couple of omelets while I brewed coffee. We didn't talk till we were sitting at the table. Then Gallin said:

"I think we need to face reality."

I nodded. "Those were the first words of the midwife to my mother after I was born."

"Funny. Now be serious."

"Which particular reality do we need to face?"

She waved her fork at me while she chewed and swallowed. "OK, listen and don't interrupt." I nodded once, sighed and sat back to listen. She went on. "Nero is dead. We have to accept that. He's gone and he ain't coming back. I deduce, but I accept it as a fact, that he was murdered by the military-industrial complex—let's call them FUCCIT for now for want of a better name—because he was opposed to them. We both knew him as well as anybody, my father knew him better than most, and we all know he would have been deeply opposed, on principal, to that institution."

"Agreed."

"So this means, one, if they killed him it was because something had come to a head. Perhaps Saul's investigation had provoked a crisis of some sort. Something that Saul had discovered maybe, and Nero and Sir John intended to expose it, along with Saul's killer."

I took a deep breath and drummed my fingers on the

table. "It follows, I grant you that. But I would need to think it through a few times. It's a lot of assumptions."

"The alternative, Mason, is that Nero's murder, just as we start investigating Saul's, just at the point when we run down Barnes, is a coincidence. I don't buy that. Nero's murder has to be connected to our investigation."

She was right. "I don't buy it either. I agree."

"So somebody, or some bodies, within that matrix of organizations that constitute the military-industrial deep state-within-the-State, had Saul and Nero murdered—I won't dignify it with the term assassinated—because either Saul was about to expose them, or because one of their key projects was about to reach fruition, and somehow Saul had got wind of it."

"A project that had something to do with genetics and nano-technology."

She nodded. "Right."

"OK, none of this is very controversial. So far you are carrying me with you."

"Good, so let's take the next step. And that is that ODIN is now our enemy."

"Shit."

"If they made a move so bold as to murder Nero, one of the most powerful men in DC, in the whole of the United States of America, it was because it was part of a coup and they had somebody else to put in his place. Somebody sympathetic to their cause."

I ran my fingers through my hair and tried to assimilate what she was telling me. "That would mean ODIN is out to hunt us down and take us out."

"That is the logical conclusion, Mason. But that is just the start."

I frowned. A sudden hiss outside told me the rain had started again. "What do you mean?"

She screwed up her paper napkin and dropped it on her plate.

"OK, granted that the best defense is always an effective attack, we have to be aware here that the sheer size and power of our enemy makes an effective attack almost impossible." She raised a hand, anticipating an argument I wasn't actually going to make. "I know," she said, "David and Goliath, but in our case Goliath is a dwarf in a pink tutu compared with the relative size of the military-industrial complex in relation to us."

"No argument."

"Good, so irrespective of what we do, or do not do, with regard to Saul and Nero's murders, what we really need to be thinking about, and fast, is how we escape, and where do we go. Because we can no longer live in the Western world and expect to survive."

"Jesus, Gallin!"

She shrugged. "Think it through."

I thought it through.

It wasn't the kind of thing you could think through in a few seconds. So I sat staring at my coffee and thinking about the various ways the entire behemoth of the military-industrial complex could be brought to heel, or at the very least brought under the scrutiny of Congress, so that Saul's and Nero's killers could be brought to justice. The obstacles seemed insurmountable, but no less inconceivable were the possible consequences for national security. The integrity of the federal state, the sanctity of its democratic system—flawed as it was—the rights and liberties of its people, all depended for their survival on the very cancer that was threatening to kill them. I had never wished so fervently for the guidance of Nero's gigantic intellect. Nor had I ever missed so deeply the sense of security you got from his towering arrogance and his enormous ego.

And while I stared into the blackness of my coffee cup, Gallin dialed her phone. She said, "May I speak to Sir John, please? This is Captain Aila Gallin." I looked up, startled, frowned and shrugged a "what the hell are you doing?" question at her.

She blinked a blink that didn't say anything. Into the phone she said, "Sir John, good morning. I hope you don't mind my calling out of the blue like this..." She smiled and gave an appreciative laugh at whatever his reply was. "I imagine you are acquainted with the developments across the pond..." She bit her lip and nodded at me. "Yeah, it was a big shock, especially for Alex. They were pretty close, you know. Of course, and I hope you don't mind me saying so, but this raises certain important issues for the Mossad..." She winked at me and waited, listening. "Well, the precise nature of the concerns I would rather not discuss over the telephone. But obviously my continued work with Alex Mason is one issue we would need to discuss."

He spoke for a while and her eyes became slightly glazed. After a moment she blinked slowly and said, "As I say, some things are best discussed in person, but if the working relationship needs to change in light of the new developments, that is something we would understand; and if you need any assistance in making those changes, naturally the Mossad would be very happy to assist in any way we can. What we need to know is that Israel's interests are being looked after by our friends, whether they are old friends or new friends. Have I been too vague, Sir John?"

She smiled and nodded. "So when would it be convenient to meet?" She shook her head and chuckled. "No, not in your office, if you don't mind, Sir John. Shall we say the Italian Gardens, by the Serpentine, in Hyde Park? This afternoon at three o'clock will be fine."

She hung up and smiled at me. I didn't smile back. "You are offering to assassinate me for Sir John?"

"It's what allies do. They help each other out."

"So what did he say?"

"He said no decision had been taken as yet regarding what should happen to our investigation or our partnership."

"So, according to him they haven't decided to kill me yet. But you nudged them along by stressing that Nero and I were close."

She gave a single nod. "Got it in one." And after a moment she added, "I have a plan."

"I'm not sure how much of a comfort that is."

"Come on, help me clear the plates and I'll explain while we wash."

# FOURTEEN

Three PM in the Italian Gardens in Hyde Park in September in the rain is a beautiful sight to behold, in a movie or on TV. In reality, the creeping chill and the damp distract you from the visual aesthetics. Both the shelter of the summer house affair at the end of the gardens, and the Italian Gardens Café just behind it, suggested themselves as obvious places for me to wait. But the risk of being seen and recognized was too great, so instead I had to lurk in the murk beneath the huge chestnut tree that towers over the Two Bears Fountain, just outside the gardens.

I had arrived an hour early, wearing a hoodie and dark shades, and installed myself under the tree on a folding chair, with a book to keep me company. Also keeping me company was Gallin's occasional chatter, which reached me through the earpiece I had in my ear, under my hood. She was discretely wired for sound with the latest cutting-edge technology from the Mossad. The nano-phones, as opposed to a mere microphone, were installed in her stud earrings and communicated with the receiver attached to my earphones via a nano-SIM.

Gallin arrived at two fifty. I watched her stroll into the gardens through the west gate and turn right, to amble through the drizzle down toward the fountain that sits in the water at the top of the Serpentine. There she leaned on the balustrade, looking out at the water.

Sir John must have been waiting, watching for her, because almost immediately he entered by the east gate and, after gazing at a few flowerbeds, he made his way to the same balustrade and stood just behind Gallin. His voice came to me loud and clear.

"It's beautiful, isn't it? Even in this horrid weather. It's not even the abundance of green. Umberto Eco said, you know, that England was not a colorful country. Because the only color was green. The real beauty is an unseen one."

Gallin's voice: "An unseen beauty? Are you philosophizing at me, Sir John?"

"I hope not." He was quiet for a moment. "It's the antiquity of it. These gardens are all of a hundred and fifty years old, but the park itself was established by Henry VIII, in 1536, just as his seven-year Reformation Parliament was coming to a close. He was of course the true father of modern parliamentary democracy. It was a fact that Saul never tired of repeating. He used to say that neither the Americans nor the British fully appreciated the common root of liberty that ran through this small island. It is fitting that freedom of speech should be enshrined here in Speaker's Corner." He added absently, "Saul was a great Anglophile, you know."

There was a protracted silence. I inched forward on my

folding chair to get a better look, and saw that Gallin had turned to face him and was leaning with her elbow on the balustrade.

"The father of parliamentary democracy? Is that something that is important to you, Sir John? The safekeeping of democracy?"

He didn't answer straight away, but I saw him move forward and place his hands on the balustrade beside her. He seemed to look out at the water for a moment.

"It's Greek, of course, though our own democracy is rooted in Norse tribalism, really. *Demos*, the people, and *kratia*, power..." He lingered on the word, as though examining it with his mind. "The people, whoever they are, never really have power, do they? Power, in order to be of any use, needs to be focused from end to end. It must come from a singular source and go to a singular source. That is why the Crown is so important. We take the dissipated power of the people and we focus it through the Crown. The Crown acts, if you like, as a lens."

"I had no idea you were a political philosopher, Sir John."

"No, well, I'm not really. But your father and I have had some good conversations in our time, at his club and at mine."

"Nero is dead. How does that affect the focusing of the power of the people?"

"Shall we walk?"

"No, let's stay right here. The sound of the water sooths me."

"Yes, I see. Well, everything depends, of course, on whom they put in his place. Nero was a very powerful man who had a lot of influence. I know there were…" He paused, hesitated over the right word. "There were *bodies*, shall we say? Bodies within the state, visionaries, who believe that democracy is a failed experiment, or at best a system that has been outgrown by technology. That technology is the next stage in human evolution, and democracy has been rendered obsolete."

"How's that?"

"Well," again he faltered, "technology will replace the Crown, or the Executive, as the lens by which the power of the people is channeled and focused."

"Technology…?"

"Well, the advent of nano-technology, Captain, suddenly makes things we used to dismiss as science fiction, like neural mapping and genetic engineering, fairly straightforward. Efficiency and obedience become potential commodities to be purchased for your particular work force or population. Of course, Nero was deeply, viscerally opposed to such visions of the future."

"So they killed him."

"We must assume so."

"What's the word at ODIN?"

"You know I can't tell you that. Why don't you ask Mr. Mason?"

She was quiet for a moment. I could hear the soft drumming of her knuckles on the wall, and from where I sat I could see the small movements of her arms.

"Mr. Mason is what is worrying me. I, and my superiors at the Institute, fear we are being drawn into something we don't fully understand. There is a lot of loose talk out there about the 'deep state' engineering a coup in Washington and

Mason and me being used as window dressing; or worse, being set up as fall guys. I don't give a damn what you do to Mason, he's your man. But you try to set me up for a fall, and you and whoever replaces Nero will be burned. We look after our own, Sir John."

"Please, my dear girl—"

"Don't patronize me, Sir John. I have cut more throats than you've had women in your bed. I am not your dear girl. I hope I am getting through to you."

"Loud and clear. What is it precisely you want, Captain Gallin?"

"One, we—that's me, my father and the boys back in Yafo—want to know what is going down at ODIN in DC, we want to know who killed Nero and why, and, two, we want to know why you asked Mason and me to investigate Saul's death."

"That is a lot to ask."

"Yeah? We are prepared to give you something in exchange."

He took his time to answer. "What can you offer?"

"If Mason has become a liability for you, we have him and we can take him out."

"You're very blunt, Captain."

"Apparently I am about as blunt as you are evasive. I don't want to do the job and then you turn around and say, 'Oh, dear me! That wasn't what I meant!'"

There was a soft grunt, then Sir John said, "Why does it matter to you what's going on at ODIN in Washington?"

"Forgive me saying so, Sir John, but that is a stupid question. Nero was a good friend to Israel, and a close personal friend of my father's. The deep state in Washington has also traditionally been a friend to us. But now suddenly they are killing their own? And taking this action without talking to friends and allies? Who is behind this? Who is moving it? Who is next? It's not so long ago the USA had a Muslim president. Do I need to spell it out?"

"No, you are very clear."

"So, you want to get off the damn fence and commit to this conversation? Or do I have to shoot you?"

There was no reply. From where I sat I could see his tall, willowy form staring out over the water, and her staring up at him. Finally I heard him sigh.

"This is beyond my jurisdiction—"

"Bullshit. I know how far your powers extend. You can order a hit on Mason, and you can give us the information we're asking for. If anything, you have more freedom of action than even Nero had because you are not tied to the powers behind the throne."

Another heavy sigh. "All right, I don't want Mason killed. I want him brought to me. I would like to talk to him. As to your other questions, the fact is I don't know who killed Nero. You probably know more about that than I do." He hesitated. "By the way..."

"What?"

"How did you know he was dead?" She didn't answer. After a moment he said, "The police never got to hear about it. Only the head office knew, and they weren't informing field operatives."

Finally Gallin said, "If you're asking whether we killed him, the answer is no. If you're asking how we knew, the answer is we are good at what we do. So what's going on in DC, Sir John? Is there a coup going down? Is the deep state going to take over? Are we looking at a fascist, technologically driven dictatorship in the United States?"

He laughed suddenly. "Wasn't that what I brought you in to find out? Wasn't that what Saul was investigating? It seems to me that I have tasked you with a mission, and you are asking me to do it for you! Brother against brother, father against son. Nobody knows whom they can trust."

She didn't answer for a moment. Then she said, "Was that what you brought us in for? I'm not so sure. You want Mason, what will you give me in return?"

His answer surprised me, and Gallin's silence said it had taken her off guard too.

"I will arrange for a meeting between you and the CEO of FUCCIT. As far as he is concerned it will have nothing to do with Saul's murder. So be careful how you proceed. Play your cards right and you may be able to acquire valuable information."

"Did you give Saul this break?"

"Something similar. Is the deal acceptable to you?"

"Yeah, I think so. Let me run it by the people back home and I'll get back to you."

I collected up my folding chair and, as I listened to Sir John wish Gallin a pleasant evening, I set off along the path toward Kensington Gardens. At Kensington Palace Gardens, otherwise known as Embassy Row, I hailed a black cab and told him to take me to Holland Park, to the High Street Kensington entrance. He dropped me there ten minutes later and I walked up through the drizzle, past the Design Museum and the sports field, and the open-air opera house, to the café. I got myself a cheese and ham baguette and a cappuccino, and found a corner table where I could sit and be damp in peace.

Gallin showed up five minutes later, ordered herself a cappuccino and a big, sticky cake and came and joined me.

"He's a sly bastard," she said as she sat opposite me. "He didn't incriminate himself at all. On the contrary, he made like he was looking out for you."

I watched her a moment, then said, "Hello."

"What are your thoughts?"

I put the last bit of baguette into my mouth and chewed. "I think he's a sly bastard, he knew we were fishing and that's why he didn't incriminate himself."

"Hmm..." She cut her carrot cake with a fork, then picked up the piece she'd cut and put it in her mouth. "That, or he's on the level. Remember. He said they don't want you dead. They want to talk to you."

"That is not as reassuring as you might think."

She chewed and watched me for a while, while I sipped and watched her back. In the end she said, "What do you want to do?"

What I wanted was to ask Nero for his advice. I shrugged and said, "We have no choice. We make the trade. I talk to them. We make sure it's in a secure location where I can get away fast if I need to. Then we go and meet Mr. FUCCIT. Come to think of it, we demand to see Mr. FUCCIT before I go and talk to them."

She nodded and turned her attention back to her cake. "Yeah," she said, "OK, that's good."

"You really think he's on the level?"

She shrugged. "I wouldn't go that far. But I got the

impression he was as keen to know what was going down as we were."

I thought about it and decided I agreed. I leaned back in my chair and asked her, "Did you get that same feeling when we spoke to him in his office?"

She looked surprised and stared at the wall a moment, then said, "No."

"Neither did I. Something has changed since then. Is it just Nero's death?"

"Maybe Elon Musk and the Skunk Works have joined forces with Mark Zuckerberg to invade people's brains with nanobots."

"The ones that were injected with Bill Gates's vaccines?" She half-smiled and I half-smiled back. I sighed. "OK, we take a stroll to the parking lot. That'll make it a little more than an hour since you spoke to him. You call him and you tell him they can talk to me..." I trailed off, thinking. "... where?"

"El Vino, on the Strand. It's always full of lawyers."

I nodded. "OK. El Vino. But you make it clear you want to talk to the CEO of FUCCIT first. Will he go for it?"

She drained her cup and looked at the dregs at the bottom while she licked the foam from her upper lip. "I guess that depends on what they want, Mason. If all they really want is to talk to you, they'll go for it. If they want more, they'll do one of two things; they'll say no, or they'll say yes and then ambush us."

"Right. So we need to be ready for the ambush."

"We will be."

As if by some telepathic accord we both stood and made our way out into the park. A cold wind had whipped up and was driving small droplets of rain like tiny, frozen bullets into any exposed flesh it could find. We tightened our coats and, scanning for anyone who might be following us, we moved into the woodlands that make up most of Holland Park. We trod the uneven, muddy paths under the huge, overarching trees, populated by peacocks, rabbits and squirrels, and came finally to the small parking lot, where the Skoda Octavia sat, as dull and gray as the sky above her.

We climbed in the car and Gallin called Sir John. He answered and she said, "Looks like we have a deal."

There was a smile in his voice. "That was quick."

"Yeah, your offering us access to the corporation swung it. But there are conditions."

"What conditions?"

"We talk to the CEO of FUCCIT first, after that you have access to Mason."

He seemed to think about it, then asked, "What kind of access?"

She sounded irritated, like he was making problems. "What kind of access do you want? You said you wanted to ask him questions. So we meet, you ask him questions."

"Where?"

"El Vino, on the Strand." He didn't say anything. "What's your problem, Sir John? I told you, if you want him taken out we'll take care of it. Otherwise you get to talk to him and you leave him to us."

"He has value for you?"

"What do you think? He was Nero's right-hand man."

"All right. I'll get back to you and we'll fix times and dates."

He hung up. Gallin pressed the starter and we moved out of the parking lot onto Abbotsbury Road.

# FIFTEEN

THE CALL CAME AS WE WERE PARKING IN THE garage at East Acton Lane. She put it on speaker and left the phone on the dash.

"Captain Gallin?"

"Yeah, who's this, please?"

"My name is Richard Chen, I represent Lord Cavendish of Norshire."

"That's nice for you. But so far you haven't told me anything."

There was a hint of a patronizing smile in the voice when he said, "Lord Cavendish is the chief executive officer of the Foundation for Computer and Cybernetic Information Technology."

"FUCCIT."

"I beg your pardon?"

"It's the acronym for your company, Dick. F-U-C..."

"Yes, I see. It hadn't occurred to me."

"Right, how can I help you, Dick?"

"Lord Cavendish understands you would like an interview with him. Would you like to make an appointment now?"

"Yeah—"

"Would tonight be convenient?"

"I don't know, where and when?"

"At our offices on Cannon Street. IT House, opposite Boots the Chemist and Cannon Street Station."

"I know it."

"You will both come?"

"Both?"

He sighed audibly. "You and Mr. Mason."

She glanced at me. I nodded. She said, "Yes."

"Top floor, and ask for me. Say, nine PM?"

"Nine PM."

"You have a sense of humor, Captain," he said with no amusement at all. "That's a good thing." I expected him to add, "You're going to need one," but he didn't. He hung up instead. Gallin picked up her phone, stared at it a moment, chewing her lip, and then looked at me. "This is it," she said, and three simple words never carried so much meaning.

---

THE WEST END OF LONDON is packed at night. The City, the so-called Square Mile, less so. The City, which lies slightly to the east of the West End, is composed mainly of banks and other financial institutions. There are a few wine bars and pubs, and a scattering of restaurants, but after five PM the City goes pretty quiet. When we got to Cannon

Street Gallin parked in front of IT House, on double yellow lines and half on the sidewalk, and put a sign on the windshield that said she had special dispensation from Whitehall to park wherever she pleased.

"I stole it," she said when she saw me staring. "Guy from the Antiterrorist Squad. He wanted to make it with me. I got him drunk and stole his pass."

I felt a strange twist of heat in my gut and asked, like I didn't really care, "And did he make it with you?"

She was opening the door to get out and stopped dead. "Come on, Mason! You know I'm saving myself for you."

I rolled my eyes and got out.

IT House was a tall tower of steel and glass, like a miniature Manhattan skyscraper. It stood opposite Cannon Street Station, independent, unattached to other buildings, with a dark alleyway either side. The main entrance to the tower was of thick plate glass, smoked to a bronze color and framed in stainless steel. It took ugliness to new depths. It stood open and invited us to a cold, green marble interior. A doorman in uniform asked us where we were going, he checked our names on a list and told us, "Eighteenth floor." He pointed to two shiny, steel elevators and added, "The lift on your right is the even numbers. I'll phone up and let them know you're on your way."

We rode the elevator to the eighteenth floor and stepped out into a broad reception area with royal blue carpets, a large, highly polished mahogany reception desk, several nests of armchairs and sofas gathered around coffee tables, and lots of potted palms. The place was dark, aside from a couple of limpid spots in the ceiling. I walked to the middle of the floor and looked around. Gallin stayed by the elevator.

A door opened over on my right, making me turn. Light leaned out of the open room, making a stencil of the person in the doorway and stretching his shadow across the floor.

"Mr. Mason, Captain Gallin. Forgive the reception. All the sensible people have gone home. Will you come in?"

As I approached the stencil resolved itself into a man with slightly Oriental features who, though in his forties, still looked boyish with a slim figure and floppy hair. He was dressed in a blue, double-breasted blazer and gray pants and managed to look smart instead of elegant. I remembered Nero telling me once that smart people work, elegant people have smart people work for them. Gallin came up beside me.

"You Richard Chen?"

"At your service, Captain."

"Lord Cavendish here?"

"He is waiting for you in his office." He gestured with his hand. "This way, please."

We followed him through a large empty space with black marble floors and a plate-glass wall peppered with the million lights of the London skyline under a dense ceiling of infernal orange clouds. Thirty feet across this space was a black glass desk with a computer on it, and to the left of the desk there was a set of tall, walnut doors. It was surreal and messed with your sense of perspective. The only purpose to the room seemed to be to be able to say, *I can piss around with some of the most expensive real estate on the planet, just for fun.*

Chen knocked on the door. It opened all on its own and he gestured inside. "Please..."

I went in first and Gallin came in after me. The office was like an echo of the antechamber, only on a grand scale.

The ceiling was high and amber lamps set in the corners managed, instead of illuminating the room, to enhance the shadows. The floor was a highly polished black marble, like the antechamber, but where that room was unfurnished, in this one, black leather armchairs stood around a highly polished mahogany coffee table, inches from the plate-glass wall that overlooked the Thames and Southwark Cathedral.

On my right, half-lost in the shadows, was a long black table with twelve chairs and a very bright silver candelabra. Beyond it I could see nothing.

In front of me, ten or twelve paces away, was a desk bizarrely at odds with the room. It was large and ornate, and two got you twenty it was at least five hundred years old. Behind it was the kind of chair Darth Vader would have over the top, all black leather and shiny chrome.

There was nobody sitting at the desk, so the voice came as a surprise.

"What do you want, Mr. Mason?"

The acoustics of the vast, marble space made it impossible to locate the source of the voice.

"For a start I'd like to see who I am talking to."

His voice carried a shade of contempt. "I'm right here, in plain view." He moved, started walking toward me. He'd been standing in the corner, looking out of the vast window at the wet city. "You don't set your aspirations very high."

"Yeah? Maybe you overrate your ability to know people."

He had reached the chair and placed his hands on the back of the headrest. "I doubt it," he said softly.

He was surprisingly young, not more than thirty-five. His hair was short, he wore jeans and what looked like hand-made, leather hiking boots, a sweatshirt and a linen jacket that was probably Armani.

"Sir John informs me that before you speak to him, you want to speak to me. I don't know what you hope to achieve with this, but here I am."

He sat, put his elbows on his desk, laced his fingers and rested his chin on them. I said, "I want a chair. And I want another for my partner."

"Really? You think it will take that long?"

I didn't answer, but after a moment Chen showed up from out of the shadows wheeling two black leather chairs. I sat and Gallin sat beside me.

"You own Sir John?" I asked.

He made the kind of expression that tells you you're keeping someone from their dinner. He gave a small shrug. "Own? What does it mean, exactly? The freedom to use something? The freedom to prevent other people from using it? If that is owning than yes, I probably do own Sir John, and most other people on the planet." Gallin snorted but he ignored her. "Or is owning the legally enshrined right to do as you will with something? In that case Sir John and you are free individuals. Where exactly does this get you, Mr. Mason?"

I started speaking without knowing exactly why, or how I could be so sure of what I was saying; but it suddenly made sense to me and I needed to say it.

"Saul Epstein had found a source of information. And for all his faults, you sure as hell didn't own him. He was a hundred times the man you are." I gave a small snort, an echo of the one Gallin had given a moment before. "Lord Cavendish, you aren't fit to lick the soles of Saul Epstein's shoes. He knew the risks he was taking, he knew the dangers he faced coming up against you, but he saw beyond his own flawed existence in a way you can't even dream of doing. He saw what you were planning to do to humanity. And he did the only thing he knew how. He prepared to tell the people."

He leaned back into the shadows and I leaned forward and pointed at him. I smiled. "I am willing to bet you don't often kill people..."

He tried to bite back the words, but I had needled him. "Don't bet too rashly, Mr. Mason."

I dismissed the threat with a wave of my hand. "Nah, but you have two very good reasons not to go around killing your opponents willy-nilly. The first is the very same reason you don't go around invading every country that has resources you need, the way you used to in the good old days. And that is because you do *not* own everybody. Your power is illusory and rests in your hands by virtue of a very delicate balancing act.

"And I'll tell you why. The problem is people. This vast population of eight billion people is out of control. You can own some of the people all of the time, and you can own all of the people some of the time... But you can't own everybody all of the time, and that means that every breach of the law that you commit, exposes you to some level of risk. And *that*, Lord Cavendish, is why you hide in the shadows. Because that gray, amorphous mass of people, if mobilized, can take you down."

He smirked at his hands like I'd said something amusing. I laughed:

"Oh, right, who is going to try and mobilize them? Who is going to be that stupid? But again, it's all smoke and mirrors. And that was another thing Saul had discovered. That there were people, in Congress, in the White House, in Parliament in the UK and in other countries, people who were not prepared to follow you into your dystopian nightmare. But nobody was mobilizing them, because they were too scared."

He shifted in his chair and his eyes were two malevolent diamonds. His voice was barely a whisper. "Fantasy."

I looked at Gallin and gave her a private smile for him to see. She returned it and mocked him with her eyes.

"Is that why you killed him? Because he was researching a fantasy?"

"You say we—"

I didn't let him finish. "So the fact that you killed him, and then you killed a man of the stature of Nero, two very high-risk targets one after another—the fact that you did that tells me one thing very clearly. You are panicking."

He didn't laugh. He should have laughed, but he didn't and Gallin stepped right in. "And if you are panicking that means, what? It means that Saul had connected with some very powerful opponents of your military-industrial fraternity, people who agreed with Eisenhower and put democracy and personal liberties above the power of the state."

I added, "And that was a real danger to you. It meant that unless you acted swiftly and decisively—some might say rashly—your seventy-five-year-old *fantasy* of world domination could collapse in a heap around your ears, wrapped in the tatters of a repealed National Security Act."

He looked from me to Gallin and back again. He spoke from the shadows but his voice was strong and calm.

"Insane conspiracy theories like this one are a penny a

dozen. Our books are audited, our accounts are scrupulously maintained, all our projects and all our research are open to government scrutiny. I really don't know what you hope to achieve with this interview."

I laughed and looked at my watch. "I understand. It's half-past nine at night. You are one of the richest men on the planet, and one of the most powerful men on the planet. The last thing you need is to be sitting in your *Blade Runner* office, discussing crazy conspiracy theories with the likes of me."

I paused and allowed the silence to close in on us, holding his eye. Then I spread my hands. "And yet...here you are. And I'll tell you why we are still here. It's because you haven't got his program, or even his research." I stabbed a finger at him. "You *know* that somebody was feeding him information that was beyond classified—information about the functioning of the deep state in Washington, information that showed how FUCCIT had become the lens that focused the power of the various defense corporations, IT, the armed forces and, more recently, nano-technology and genetics.

"But they weren't just feeding him information. They were feeding him *probative* information. Information you could not ignore or dismiss." I paused. "And you think I know who his informant was, and where the information is. And *that* is why you are still here listening to my crazy conspiracy theory."

The huge room was very silent, and very still, and eventually his silence became the very admission he was trying to avoid by saying nothing. That realization dawned on him and he sighed. "And do you?"

I gave an annoyingly self-satisfied chuckle. "I am going to answer your question, Lord Cavendish. So bear with me. But before I do, I am going to explain something to you that I figure nobody has ever told you till now. You are an arrogant son of a bitch with a God complex and an ego so vast it blocks everything else from view. This is a problem because it doesn't let you see just how smart other people can be. Now let me point out a couple of things to you that you need to know. I am smart, and so is Captain Gallin, but Nero? Nero was Einstein smart. He was a real genius. Now this raises two questions for you: one, would a man that smart allow Saul's documentary to be stolen that easily? Let me explain that. Assuming that Nero was behind our investigation, assuming he brought the team together, knowing what was at stake, would he be *that* careless about allowing the documentary to be stolen?

"And two, even if he disregarded his own safety, which he never did, would he put his two chief operatives in a position where simple torture would elicit the whereabouts of the documentary and the research, and the names of his contacts?"

He clenched his brow and gave his head a little twitch.

"Are you throwing me a curveball, Mr. Mason? What is this sudden introduction of Nero?"

I put a smile on my right cheek and tried to penetrate the shadows to read his expression. "So, there are things you don't know and people you cannot reach after all."

He sighed. "You said you were going to answer my question. So far all you have done is play word games. Do you have the documentary, and do you know who Saul's source was?"

And as he asked them, the answer to those questions dawned on me. "The answer to both is yes," I said. "And I'd say your questions are an admission of guilt."

"Guilt?" He looked like the word amused him. "I asked you when you came in here what you wanted. So far you still haven't told me. Now I am asking you again."

"I'm selling, Lord Cavendish. Are you buying?"

"That depends on the price—and on what precisely you are selling."

"I'm selling a three terabyte pen drive with the complete documentary and all the research that went into it, plus contacts, how the contacts were made and where and when they met. That includes Deep Throat and the precise nature of Nero's involvement."

I could feel Gallin's eyes boring into my head in the semi-darkness, asking herself if I was bullshitting or if I had been holding out on her. I told myself she should know me well enough by now to know I was bullshitting and ignored her. Cavendish narrowed his eyes at me.

"Why?" he asked simply.

I leaned forward and spoke to him like he was an idiot. "Because, Cavendish, people are not as stupid as you think they are! And you are not as powerful as you like to think you are. But I am not so stupid as to think that one man on his own can bring you down." I sat back and crossed one leg over the other. "Faced with a situation like that, a smart man joins an enemy who is too strong to defeat."

He leaned forward into the light, with his eyebrows arched high. "*Joins?*"

"I want in." I gestured at Gallin. "We both want in. We want to be part of the club. And for that we are going to need a couple of billion bucks each. Tell me what I'm selling isn't worth it."

He nodded at his fingertips, laid neatly along the edge of his desk. "Oh, it's worth it," he said. "I'm just not sure you are."

# SIXTEEN

Gallin said, "What the hell is that supposed to mean?"

He looked past us and spoke into the darkness. "Tell Leo to come in, will you, Richard?"

I heard echoing, marble footsteps behind me as Cavendish picked up a sleek black phone. He punched one button, and sank back in his chair. "Yeah, Eye, I'm here with him now and he doesn't know shit. Neither does she. They are giving me a lot of eyewash about taking out insurance, but this was just a fishing expedition." He listened for a bit, running his fingers along the edge of the table, as though seeking a hidden button. After a moment he said, "I'll take them for a talk with Mr. Smith just in case. But I think we're wasting our time." A spasm of irritation crossed his face. "Yes, I know *somebody* killed them! But Mason doesn't know who."

His eyes found mine and then Gallin's. He knew he'd

had a slip of the tongue, and I knew it didn't matter because he was going to kill us anyway. I had heard the soft tread of boots behind us, and now I heard the cocking of at least a dozen weapons. He hung up and I said:

"If we don't check in, in twenty—"

"Stop." He stared me right in the eye. "It's a lie. I know it, you know it. You heard me. This was a very amateur fishing expedition born of desperation, and you caught a great white shark. You caught Jaws."

Gallin snapped, "Who's Mr. Smith?" When she saw he wasn't going to answer she added, 'I know *somebody* killed them...?' You're full of shit. You're completely in the dark. You know nothing."

He spoke past her. "Get them out of here. Take them to the Gateway. Advise Mr. Smith we need him there."

We were dragged to our feet, cuffed and shoved unceremoniously out of the big, black room. The doors closed behind us and I had a look around. There were six guys around Gallin and six around me. They all had semi-automatics and they all had that "shit-shave-and-a-shoe-shine" smartness that comes with mercenaries from the southern hemisphere. They can murder you in a hundred and sixty different ways without batting an eyelid, and they won't get a drop of blood on their shoes or muff the crease in their pants.

They led us to a service elevator and we rode down to the garage. I was kicking myself internally for having allowed us to get trapped so easy. Gallin caught my eye and there was nothing cocky or smart about her expression. We were in big trouble and we both knew it. The kind of trouble you'd can't smart-ass your way out of. And the worst part was that the only person who was ever going to help us, was the one standing next to us.

I winced and asked, "You guys open to be bribed?"

A guy with short blond hair, blue eyes and a cravat, and a face like well-groomed concrete, said, "One more crack and I'll beat you into an unconscious pulp."

I nodded and decided I needed to conserve my strength so I could kill him later.

We came out into the parking garage. It was practically empty. Two guys went off into the shadows carrying keyless fobs. Two bleeps echoed in the cavernous darkness, and they made their way toward two dark SUVs that were flashing among the columns.

They came back in a small convoy of two Audi SUVs. Gallin was dragged into the rear truck and I was dragged into the one in front. A dark cloth bag was pulled violently over my head and tied tight around my throat. I took a deep breath and set about meditating and making peace with myself, trying to remember what Sir Roger Penrose had said, that nobody ever dies out of their own experience of life. You may die out of the lives of the people around you, and they may die out of yours. But you never die out of your own experience.

I tried to take comfort from that, and told myself that if Gallin was born into my next life...

But I trailed off because that part of my mind that doesn't give a damn if I live or die, as long as I do my job properly, had started analyzing the sounds I was hearing from outside: the echoing foghorns, the barges, the sounds of the river.

I noticed there was practically no traffic. And all the

while our progress was the same: we went straight, then hit a traffic circle—what the Brits call a roundabout—then we'd go straight again and hit another roundabout, then straight —roundabout. No sharp rights, no sharp lefts.

If it had been just that I would eventually have become disoriented anyway, but all the while the sounds of the river stayed on my right. So that meant we were moving east, downriver toward the sea, toward Essex and the mouth of the Thames.

We drove for a little more than an hour. I soon gave up trying to keep track of the turns and circles we went through. But I stayed focused on the relative position of the river. At first it was easy to identify, but as we moved out of London the sounds became more distant and sporadic. Though they were always on my right. Then, after a little less than an hour they became more frequent again, and louder. We were arriving at a port.

That was what he had meant by the Gateway. We were at the port at Corringham, in Essex, at the mouth of the Thames. The port they called the Gateway to London. For some reason the thought made me feel slightly sick. It might be its remoteness, it might be the ease with which you can dispose of a body out there, or it might be the easy access to deep, cold oceans.

Maybe it was all three.

We slowed, turned right and right again, a couple of twists and turns and we came to a halt. The front passenger door opened. I heard a steel shutter being lifted. Then the car door slammed and we were moving again. The tires screamed and echoed in some kind of large, enclosed space, and we came to a halt just before the engine died.

Next thing, the door was wrenched open beside me and I was grabbed and dragged from the vehicle. Somebody pulled the hood off my head and in the dim light I saw we were in a parking garage. There were four or five cars parked in random spaces, and I spotted among them the dark SUV into which they had bundled Gallin. That gave me a jolt of adrenalin, though whether it was fear or hope, I wasn't sure.

They dragged me across the filthy, rubber and oil-blackened floor and shoved me into an elevator. We rose two floors and slowed to a halt. The doors hissed open and they dragged me out into a large, open space. It must have been one and a half thousand square feet. It was reminiscent of the offices we had just left, but where they had been slick and evil, this was just abandoned and disused, shabby and dilapidated.

The only light came from the glass wall opposite the elevators, which overlooked a large parking lot with tall, spindly streetlamps and no cars. The place was not furnished. Except that there were two bentwood chairs in the middle of the floor. I saw them and the feeling of nausea I'd had before came back with a vengeance. The best thing this setup offered was a rapid death. And I knew that was very unlikely.

They shoved me toward one of the chairs. I knew I was about to cross a point of no return. Once they got the duct tape out it would be curtains. I glanced around. They knew what I was thinking. This was my last chance to take them and try to escape. There were six of them with guns. The closest was eight feet away. If I made a move now, I wouldn't last fifteen seconds. As I looked at them in turn I told myself, it might be better to go down fighting than endure what they had in store for me, but the one thing that held me back was Gallin. I couldn't leave her to face this alone.

They shoved me onto the chair, removed my cuffs and duct-taped my wrists to the sides of the chair. Then they stood around in a semi-circle, ready to turn me into a colander if I moved.

A couple of minutes passed and the other half of the gang came in. There was Lord Cavendish followed by Richard Chen, and I wasn't all that surprised to see behind them Sir John. I had figured already that he was Mr. Smith.

Behind him came six guys with guns and Gallin. They shoved her onto the chair slightly to my right, removed her cuffs and bound her the same way they had bound me. Somebody brought Sir John a chair and he sat opposite me, about fifteen or twenty feet away. He had no expression on his face and he said nothing.

Cavendish strutted into the middle of the floor, looking down first at me and then at Gallin. Something about his walk, about the Levi jeans, the sweatshirt and the Armani jacket was wrong. I couldn't put my finger on it, but I was just telling myself that, wherever he had learned to dress like that, it was not Eton or Oxford, and it certainly wasn't Cavendish Hall, or whatever his manorial estate was called.

"Let me," he said, quietly, "just explain something to you and see if I can make you understand." He held up thumb and forefinger indicating something very small. "You, both of you, are as ants—no, as fungus, *microbes*, to us." He gave a short laugh, looking up at the ceiling. "You really believe, *you really believe*—" His voice was becoming shrill, which was something else they didn't encourage in stiff-upper-lip institutions. "That *Lord Cavendish of Norshire* would stoop to meeting you? *You don't exist* for Lord Cavendish of Norshire. You, your organization, your bosses —you are *nothing!*"

I snarled unpleasantly, "So you're just a gofer, stealing the crumbs from the table, justifying your lack of dignity by exalting your boss. You're not original. What's your name?"

He took a few steps closer to me. The rage and hatred in his eyes was abnormal, born of some dark pathology of his mind. "Believe me, Mason, I wield more power today than ninety percent of the world's presidents. I have *met* Lord Cavendish, and we have spoken. He knows my name!"

It was probably ill-advised, but I couldn't suppress the laugh. "Spare us your wet dreams, Marvin. You'll end up embarrassing yourself with your hero-erotic ravings. What do you want? If you think you can get away with abducting an American government agent and a British government agent just because a chorus of angels breaks into a heavenly choir every time you think of your boss, you've got another think coming, pal."

The little speech made me feel better, but judging from Gallin's expression she wasn't thanking me for it. Vaguely I remembered that in special forces they teach you, when you're captured, to keep your mouth shut until you have a chance of escape. Until then play meek, afraid and obedient.

He stepped up and gave me a decent backhander. I checked my mouth for blood. There wasn't any. I looked up at him. "Is that how you hit your boyfriends when they get fresh?"

His face said he was going to do something ugly, but Sir John's voice cut in before he did.

"He is ignorant, Cecil, and he is too ignorant to know it. You are wasting time. Cut to the chase."

"Yeah, cut to the chase...Cecil."

Sir John cut in again. "Whom do you work for in Washington? What is your department?"

I frowned at him, and I could feel Gallin's eyes burning into his head.

I hesitated just a moment before telling him, "I work for the Pentagon," and added, "You know that."

"Yes." He gave a sigh that said he was being patient. "The Pentagon employs around twenty-seven thousand people, Mr. Mason, and that is not counting the extra-mural workers. Now, I need to know, Mr. Mason, without prevarication, precisely what department you work for, and who is your boss."

I tried to squeeze as much thinking as I could into three seconds and said, "I work for the Office of the Director of Intelligence. My direct boss is Garry Reid, and above him is the president." I glanced at Cecil and added, "I've seen a couple come and go, and spoken to all of them. But there were no celestial choirs."

Sir John snapped, "That kind of provocation will not help your cause. The chances are very high that you will both die here today, unless you can manage to be very cooperative indeed."

"I'll try to remember that. What else do you need to know?"

"Have you found Saul Epstein's work, or any material relating to it?"

"Yes."

"You took a sudden, flying visit to New York. What was that for?"

"To deliver Saul's producer into protective custody, and to place a three terabyte USB drive where it cannot be found."

"What do you know about the man called Nero?"

I forced myself to ignore Gallin. I knew if we made eye contact our confusion would show. Instead I said, "I know he works for the Office of the Director of Intelligence. He is very secretive and handles stuff above top secret. I know he's dead."

"*How* do you know he's dead?"

"Because I found his body. He'd been shot in the head."

"What was the purpose of your meeting with him?"

"He had requested that Pamela Peach-Plum be delivered to him. So that's what I did. But when we got to his office he was dead." I gave it a couple of beats and added, "I had assumed you had killed him."

"What made you assume that?"

It was a good question. Gallin answered.

"At that time it seemed to us that we were engaged in a struggle for power between the so-called deep state, or military-industrial complex, and the White House, and perhaps the executives of various other Western countries. But primarily the White House and Whitehall. It was our understanding, from what we know of Saul's research, that the Pentagon, backed by the military-industrial complex, was engaged in some kind of coup, and that the White House and Whitehall were attempting to halt it."

"A bit fantastic, perhaps."

"Yeah," I said with heavy irony, "because we have never

seen a coup before, in Britain or the United States." Gallin cut in, "The technology for it exists?"

He flashed her a look. "The technology for what?"

"We don't know yet exactly, but we know it involves genetic engineering by means of nanotechnology."

"You are simply guessing?" It was a statement but he made it sound like a question. I shook my head. "No, more of an educated guess."

He didn't seem impressed. "You say you have the documentary and his notes. How much of it have you seen?"

I smiled. "We haven't had a lot of time, but we've seen enough."

He nodded silently a couple of times, then asked, "Who was his source?"

Gallin said, "If you hadn't abducted us we'd be well on our way to finding out by now. Instead we're wasting time here."

"Where is his report?"

I laughed. "Come on! Seriously? In about half an hour it is going to initiate a long series of journeys by post all around the world, from attorneys' offices in Brasilia to remote villages in Outer Mongolia, via Turkey and the South Pacific. And you can be very sure, Sir John, that the people with instructions on what to do with it, haven't the vaguest idea who I am."

He looked away at the wall of black glass, thinking. I turned to Cyril and put a sneer in my voice. "So what have they promised you, Cyril? What fantasy are they nurturing within you? You know the first thing the new emperor does when he comes to the throne, right?"

His face was pure bile. "Nothing you can say..."

"He kills all his closest associates, because they are the people who are most dangerous to him."

"No." He was shaking his head. Gallin said, "Go back to school and read your history."

"But this time it is different!" Sir John scowled at him. Cyril's cheeks were flushed pink. "Never, never before has an empire been built on the foundations of science and technology!"

Sir John snapped, "Cyril!"

He didn't hear him, he just kept plowing on into his fantasy. "Until now social engineering has simply focused on manipulating people's subjective drives and desires. But now we can actually *design and install* those subjective drives! *We can make people want what we want them to want!*"

Sir John snapped louder, "Cyril!"

I drowned him out with "Yah, yadda yadda bullshit!" which Gallin supplemented with a loud laugh. Cyril advanced on me, growing shrill.

"Where do you think your subjective drives come from? Well? What, are they god given? Do they just appear out of the ether?"

I looked at Gallin and interrupted him. "Teach a back-street kind a word like 'subjective' and suddenly he thinks he's educated."

"*Well they don't! They are organic, generated by hormones and neurotransmitters, governed by our genetic makeup! And just as we can manufacture desires, we cann—*"

Sir John had risen and moved in quickly. Now he grabbed Cyril and spun him round. "What are you doing? What do you need to prove to this ape? Keep silence, until it is time to speak."

"Just when it was getting interesting," I said. "OK, so do we have a deal? I give you the flash drive, you let us into the club."

Cyril turned and grabbed a fistful of my hair. "You?" he said. "You serve no useful purpose. You are a liar and a fake. You die!"

# SEVENTEEN

WHAT HAPPENED NEXT TOOK ME BY SURPRISE. IT shouldn't have, but it did. I heard Gallin scream. At the same moment I saw three guys advancing on me. At first it didn't make sense. But that was only a fraction of a second. Then the plastic grocery bag and the duct tape made excellent sense. Because I saw them shove one over Gallin's head and tape it hard around her throat.

I heard horrible, inarticulate, animal sounds and knew they were Gallin's and mine. Then the bag was over my head and I was telling myself not to scream, not to breathe; and in the short seconds that followed I heard Sir John's shouts drowned out by Cecil's, and the tramp of feet as they left the room.

Then panic gripped me. In a fraction of a second I had run through all my options and knew there was no way I could get the bag off my head. My heart was pounding hard and fast, and I knew that was using up valuable oxygen.

Then I heard Gallin make an inarticulate noise between rage and fear.

I stood, not knowing what I planned to do. The chair taped to my wrists forced me to hobble, like an old man. My mind was frantic, screaming, seeking something—anything —I could use. But apart from Gallin and me the room was empty. And the seconds were draining away.

Rage and panic welled up inside me. All I could see was white plastic. My lungs were bursting. I turned left and right. My belly was burning, and the more it burned the more my lungs wanted to suck in air. I wanted to scream to Gallin that I was coming. But I wasn't. I was wasting the last few precious moment of our lives panicking.

I opened my mouth and screamed, "*Gallin!*"

And as I drew breath the bag sucked into my mouth and I began to suffocate. No air could get in and there was no air left in my lungs to blow it out. Then my brain and my body went into a crazy frenzy. I tried to bite the bag, but it was too slick. My lungs were burning in agony. I tried wildly to think of something that would hold the bag against my teeth so I could bite through. There was nothing. A wild, berserker madness filled my lungs, my belly and my brain, and I jumped.

I jumped high and came down, two hundred and twenty pounds, as badly twisted as I could. There was a horrible splintering of wood as the chair shattered under my full weight. I was growing faint, I was nauseous and my heart was thundering. I picked up a piece of wood and stabbed myself frantically and violently in the mouth. The plastic ripped and I sucked air, rasping noisily into my lungs.

Half-screaming, ripping the bag from my face, I staggered toward Gallin. I was crazy, wheezing and grunting like an animal. She was slumped and immobile in her chair. I was trailing bits of broken chair from my wrists. I grabbed one at random and perforated the bag over her head. I tore it open and peeled it away from her face. Her eyes were closed and she was pale and lifeless. Groaning and wheezing and making noises that were barely human, I patted her face, shook her, felt for her pulse and clutched her to me. All the while there was a surreal madness in my mind, a rage against these bastards who coolly decided they had the right to do such a thing to another human being.

To Gallin!

I pushed her back, about to drop her on the floor and give her artificial respiration, croaking something about, "Come on, Gallin! Breathe, baby!" She was watching me with two slightly hooded eyes.

"Son of a bitch," I croaked, laughing and scowling.

She arched an eyebrow. "How come every time you rescue me you lose your voice?" I tried several times to say something, but my throat wasn't having it. "Don't they teach you breath control at ODIN, Mason? With that enormous black budget you have, they could teach you breath control. You can probably hold your breath for a minute or more. You know how long you had the bag over your head?"

I squeaked, "No."

"About fifteen seconds. Good call with the chair, though. Are you OK?"

"No," I said again. "I want to go and kill somebody!"

"Also a good plan, but perhaps we should think it through."

"No, you've been doing pranayama or some shit, and

you're in an altered state. Thinking will take too long. We go now. We kill."

And I ran, wielding bits of a broken chair. *"Mason!"* The cry followed me out of the room, but I ignored it. The rage in me was too great, and now that I knew Gallin was OK, it was totally unleashed. I ran, making strange noises in my throat: a grunting wheezing that was only partly the lack of oxygen. The other part was primal bestiality.

Behind me I heard a crash, but failed to register that I had left Gallin taped to her chair. I could think of just one thing. I needed to get my hands on that prick Cavendish.

That, and the fact that I needed a weapon. I crossed the first big room and as I came to the door I saw a glass panel in the wall with a fire hose and an axe. I ran to it in a frenzy, aware I was yelling, but unable to stop. Grunting like a thing possessed I beat it with my fist. It didn't break So I beat it some more and finally head-butted it three times, and when the glass finally gave I reached in and grabbed the axe, and left my blood on the hanging shards.

Then I burst through the door onto the landing and listened. I could hear voices. They were disembodied, floating in the stairwell.

I had no plan. I had no idea what I intended to do. I was still living the wild terror of trying to suck in air through that indestructible, plastic barrier. The screaming panic in my lungs. I was in a fever of outrage and hatred and all I wanted was to get my hands on the bastards who had done that to us.

Then I heard Cavendish's voice. He was maybe two floors down. He was giving instructions. The words echoed and were hard to follow but I caught, "...dispose of the bodies..."

That was followed by footsteps stomping on the stairs, climbing toward me. I didn't wait for them. I took the stairs a landing at a time. I caught them outside the elevator doors. One of them was the guy who'd said he'd beat me to a pulp. They gaped, and he said, "What...?" but I was already swinging the axe in a wide arc from over my right shoulder. The broad blade bit deep into that place where the neck joins the shoulder and kept going. Blood, that looked black in that dim light, sprayed up toward the ceiling in a thick stream.

I didn't pause, I didn't make a sound. I wrenched the axe free while his terrified pal fumbled for his weapon. I smashed the head of the axe into his face, in a savage jab, and as he cupped his bleeding nose with his hands, I raised the chopper over my head and brought it crashing down, splitting his skull in two. As his legs buckled and he sank to the floor, I yanked the axe free and hurtled down the next flight of steps. I was trying to yell and scream to Cavendish to wait for me, to come and get me, but my throat had seized up in a kind of hysterical paralysis.

I clattered down, landing by landing, and found each one empty of people and furniture. Somewhere, that little part of my human brain that was still working was asking why, but ninety-eight percent of me didn't give a damn. I ran back and forth, gripping the bloody axe in both hands, searching for a sign of them, listening for their voices. Something like an instinct told me they had gone back to the parking garage. I kicked my way out of the main doors and found, on my right, the entrance to the underground parking. And as I saw it, I heard the roar of an engine, and I ran, screaming silently in my paralyzed throat.

I came to the top of the ramp and looked down at two glaring headlamps rising toward me. God alone knows what kind of diabolical silhouette they must have seen bearing down on them. I didn't pause. I raised the axe over my head and charged. I knew the driver was on my left, but I ran for the center of the car. It was only as he began to accelerate, and I was six or seven feet from the hood, that I leapt to my left and brought the axe thundering down on the windshield. A torrent of small shards of shattered glass showered the driver's face and as he let go the wheel to protect himself, I wrenched open the door and drove the axe in a big swing, up and under into his throat below his chin.

His whole body twitched uncontrollably and the SUV began to creep backward as the second SUV came up behind it. The horn screamed, but there were voices screaming over it. Then everything happened in a couple of seconds.

The back door was opening and I grabbed it and wrenched it all the way. The trunk collided with the truck coming up behind and for a moment it was immobile. The guys started to scramble out. I planted my feet and without even looking I plowed into them, swinging the axe right and left, down from above and up and under. Great showers of blood and gore erupted. Bits of limb spun in the air. My mind was full of screaming. And the more I tried to scream at them, the more my throat seized up and the more madness and frustration drove me on.

It could not have taken more than a few seconds. I looked around me and all there was, was a heap of carnage in the SUV and at my feet. I looked left and the front passenger of the rear SUV had climbed down and was training a Glock 17 on me, leaning on the door.

I opened my mouth in a huge, silent roar and leapt to the side in one giant step and swung from the waist. His weapon exploded and spat fire at me. I didn't care. The molten lead flicked past my face as the axe traveled up from the floor to the door where the weapon was resting. The guy shied away. But the blade caught the semi-automatic and ripped it from his fingers.

Then all the doors were opening. Everyone was getting out except him. He was trying to scramble back in. The blade tore into his shoulder and tore off his arm. Two or three men were falling over each other trying to scramble out the back. I decapitated one of them and as the other two fell away, shouting, I went after them, hammering at them indiscriminately, treading on them as they fell, making my way around to the other side. There I saw Sir John and Cavendish running up the ramp. Cavendish had a cell in his hand.

And now my voice came. I thundered up the ramp bellowing like a demented bull. *"You going to put a goddamned plastic bag over my head? You son of a bitch? You gonna suffocate me? You bastard? You gonna put a plastic bag over my head? You piece of—"*

Cavendish stopped and turned, waving a trembling gun at me. He was waxy pale and his voice was high and shrill as he said, "Stay away from me..."

I leered at him and snarled, "Who's insignificant now, Mr. Nobody?"

The first swing was short and sweet and took off his arm at the elbow. As he gaped at it in disbelief, I brought it back and cut through his neck. His head, still wearing an astonished face, spun, bounced when it landed on the blacktop and rolled down the ramp, into the black bowels of the parking garage.

I turned, looking for Sir John. He was on his knees beside Gallin, who was holding a gun to his head.

"Alex, stay away."

"I am not going to kill him, Gallin." I was still croaking.

"It's time to stop, Alex."

"I know what he did."

"Yes, I know what he did, too, Alex. He did it to me too. But we need him alive."

Suddenly I had that strange feeling in my nose, and my eyes were hot and I couldn't control my voice. "They killed Nero, and they were going to kill you. The bustards!"

"We need him alive, Alex. You need to start coming down. One step at a time, Alex. It's all over now, and you need to start coming down. We need to get out of here—fast, and we need to take Sir John with us, and I need to know you are not going to cut him in half."

"I couldn't breathe, Gallin, and I thought you... I thought you couldn't breathe either. I was really scared."

"OK, now I need you to get a grip. It all worked out in the end. And now I need you to come back to yourself and stop acting crazy. OK? Get a grip, Alex."

"I'm not going to kill him. Stop calling me Alex."

"The SUV at the back."

I looked back at it. "What?"

"It still has the key in the ignition. Get in, drive around the charnel house you have created, and bring the car up the ramp."

I thought about it. It was a simple enough proposition. I nodded. My brain was starting to work again. I started down the ramp but Gallin's voice stopped me.

"Mason?"

"What?"

"You don't need the axe anymore."

I looked down at it gripped in my hand. Both hands were slick with blood, as was the handle of the axe. I dropped it on the floor and climbed into the SUV. Reversing away from the shattered, disabled Audi in front of me, and then climbing that ramp was a grizzly business, but I hadn't come down from my berserker high enough yet to care much. Out on the blacktop, my door opened and Gallin leaned in.

"Get out, Mason. Get in the back. I'll drive."

"I can drive."

"Yeah, I know you can. But I need to think and I think better when I'm driving. Also I want you to do some breathing, cool off, center your thoughts. They teach you that shit, right?"

"Yeah, they teach us all that." I climbed in the back and she dragged Sir John around to the front passenger seat and shoved him in. "You'd better behave, smart ass. I for one would like to see what he'd do to you if I let him. And remember, he's sitting right behind you."

She got in behind the wheel, closed her eyes and sighed, just like a woman who has a car, a full gas tank and nowhere to go. Sir John spoke suddenly. "We need to go somewhere and talk. This is an almighty mess. This car is covered in blood. It will be on CCTV cameras all over the port. My god! What a disaster!"

"If you've got something more useful than a gripe, spill it. Otherwise shut up."

He glanced at her. "They used to have a fleet of vans and lorries here. At the eastern end of the building, around the corner, there's a yard where they used to wash and maintain the vehicles. With a bit of luck the hoses will still be functional. But you'll have to be quick. You haven't got more than ten minutes."

As we pulled away and moved toward the far end of the building, I asked, "What happens in ten minutes?"

"There will be armed police swarming all over this place like flies. We won't stand a chance."

# EIGHTEEN

Gallin stared at him with her eyes screwed up.

"*We?*"

I snapped, "Don't waste time! I need an immediate conference with the prime minister. And I need to be put through to the White House!" They both turned and stared at me, frowning like they hadn't expected me to be able to talk. "*Now!*"

Ten minutes later we were hurtling west again toward London while Gallin babbled on the phone to her father, and Sir John spoke urgently on the phone to the Home Secretary.

"Sue, I need you to listen very carefully. Yes, I know what time it is, but if I tell you this is one of the most important decisions you are ever likely to make I will not be overstating the case." You have to love the Brits. "Quite so, we are in a dark Toyota Proace Verso heading west at speed along the A13. We need immediate police escort to Downing Street...

Yes, Sue, Downing Street, where I need you and James..." He sighed quietly and said with extreme patience, "Yes, Sue, I do mean the Foreign Secretary. I need you and James and Liz—the Prime Minister—wide awake and drinking coffee. And please, get that escort in the next five minutes, we appear to be averaging a hundred and ten miles an hour."

I had pulled my phone from my pocket and sat staring at it. My mind was racing, trying to make sense of a jigsaw that seemed to have no corners and no straight edges. Gallin suddenly pounded the steering wheel with the heel of her hand and shouted, "*Will somebody please tell me what the hell is going on?*"

Nobody answered her, but the truck was suddenly filled with the sound of howling sirens. I looked out back and saw four bike cops closing in on us with their lights flashing. The lead bike pulled up alongside and Sir John opened the window and leaned out, showing the ride something in his wallet. The cop saluted and he and another took up a position in front of us, while the other two settled behind.

Sir John was busy on his phone again, dialing. I said, "You had it all along." He stopped dead and looked at me in the mirror. Then he started dialing again and put the phone to his ear. I was talking like an automaton as the pieces began to fit together in a way that still made no sense. "How could I be so stupid? You told us from the start. You told Gallin. I can remember your exact words." Gallin was staring at me in the rearview. "You said, '...I asked him several times to clarify his concerns for me, but he refused.'" I paused and laughed. "You actually said it, 'His precise words, the last time we spoke, were, *When my research is finished, you'll be the first to read it.*' Son of a bitch!"

Gallin had shifted her gaze and was staring at Sir John. He ignored us both and spoke into the phone. "Nigel, we have a code red. Deliver my briefcase to Number Ten immediately." He hung up and said, to nobody in particular, "I will clarify later. This is neither the time nor the place."

Fifteen minutes later we were rolling down Whitehall and turning in at the gates of Downing Street.

We were surrounded by cops as we clambered out, and Sir John was flashing his wallet as men in plain clothes bustled us in through the back door and hurried us upstairs. Somebody handed him a black attaché case. He took it without comment and we crossed a broad landing and were ushered then into a surprisingly large office where the Home Secretary, the Foreign Secretary and the prime minister were all sitting, staring at us. The prime minister was on the phone. When we came in she said, "They've just arrived, Gabriel. Yes, I'll tell her. We'll talk later," and she hung up.

She stayed at her desk but gestured us to a couple of armchairs and a sofa. Then she gave Sir John the kind of look that makes a man's blood turn to Slush Puppie.

"Sir John," she said, making him instantly six years old, "would you like to explain precisely why we are here, and just exactly how you come to feel you have the authority to summon the—"

"I'm afraid, Prime Minister, and forgive me for interrupting, but we simply haven't time for this. My authority comes from Section Three, subsection two of the Combined Intelligence Act, otherwise known as the ODIN Act. Perhaps you should call the Attorney General. Meanwhile you need to trigger Section Five of the Security of the Realm Act immediately and place this list of people," he paused to open his attaché case and extracted a printed list which he slipped across the desk, "under strict house arrest tonight. There is no time to lose."

She was scowling at him and took the list. It didn't take more than a couple of seconds for her to look up and say, "Are you quite out of your mind?"

"No, Prime Minister," and he stood and with a rare flash of irritation he dumped his case on her desk and snapped, "but by dawn you could be facing a military coup. This case is filled with irrefutable, conclusive proof, beyond the remotest doubt! And the men and women on that list, under the leadership of Lord Cavendish of Norshire, financed by the Foundation for Computer and Cybernetic Information Technology and a network of other Anglo-American corporations within the so-called military-industrial complex, will execute that coup! Unless you act first and place them under arrest."

Absolute silence settled on the room and something seemed to snap in my brain. I pulled out my cell and called Lovelock.

"Alex! For God's sake! What is *happening?*"

"We have a code red." The prime minister was staring at me. I held her eye and said, "Put me through to the president."

It took about three minutes. Then a hesitant voice came on the line.

"Mr. Mason...?"

"Mr. President, sir, as you have probably been told I am a senior agent at the Office of the Director of..."

"Hold on a minute there, son... I'm just...just hold on... I am going to hand you over to the vice... Kami? You want to take this? Mr. Mason, senior agent of the office of something."

A woman's voice came on the line, crisp and efficient. "This is the vice president speaking. I have received a code red notification from ODIN. Would you kindly explain to me—"

I eyed Sir John and echoed his words from a few seconds earlier.

"Ma'am, we haven't time for all that. I need you to be silent and listen to me very carefully. I am sitting here with the prime minister of Great Britain, the Home Secretary and the Foreign Secretary, as well as the head of Odin in Britain and Agent Aila Gallin of the Mossad."

"What the hell is the Mossad doing there?"

"Ma'am, I need you to listen and not talk." The prime minister had started going through the contents of the briefcase and was passing documents to the Home Secretary and the Foreign Secretary. Sir John was speaking quietly but forcefully to them. I went on, "We have here proof positive —and I mean proof beyond any shadow of a doubt—that a coup is being contemplated by leading figures within industry and defense, with a view to driving through..." I hesitated, then said it, "a new world order, ma'am, in which the democratic rule of law is replaced—made obsolete—by advanced genetics and nano-technology. Saul Epstein was murdered because he was going to expose the plot, and Nero was murdered for the same reason. And ma'am, Sir John, the head of ODIN UK, Captain Gallin and I are certain that if the coup goes ahead, it will go ahead tonight."

"You're out of your mind."

"The mastermind behind the plot is Lord Cavendish of

Norshire, and it is financed by the Foundation for Computer and Cybernetic Information Technology and corporations associated with it in the military-industrial complex."

"You are out of your tiny mind. What the hell? How did you get through to this number...?"

"Ma'am, I am going to send you a list of names, and I need you to deploy the Secret Service to put these people under house arrest and shoot them if they try to escape. This is a code red, ma'am. And while I send you the list, I am going to connect you by video with the prime minister..."

"The Foundation for Computer and Cybernetic Information Technology? F-U-C-C-I-T? Are you for real?"

"Yeah, FUCCIT Just Do It, ma'am."

I switched to video and handed the phone to the prime minister. She stared me in the face as she took it, like she was wondering what I was. I heard a small squeak from my phone, "Liz? What the hell...?"

"I'm looking at the material now, Kamala. This is not a stunt. This is real and we do not have time to prevaricate... It, um, means hesitate and put off...no, there really is no time for that."

I pulled Sir John aside and told him, "I need to get this material to Lovelock and to the Secretary of Defense so they can action it while the vice president talks about it.

While Sir John set about doing that, I heard the prime minister, like a terrifying hybrid of Head Mistress and Valkyrie, "I am *sorry*, Kamala, but we must take action! I have told you what I am going to do, and I would *not* wish to be in your shoes tomorrow morning, if Westminster emerges from this with its parliamentary democracy intact, and

Washington has tanks on the street and you and Joe are locked up in Camp David!" She went to hand me back my phone but stopped, put it back to her ear and said firmly, "FUCCIT! Just Do It!"

Then she handed me the phone. "Thank you, Mr. Mason."

"Ma'am."

Gallin, who had been talking quietly on the phone, raised her hand like a school kid. The prime minister gazed at her a moment.

"Yes, Captain Gallin?"

"Prime Minister, Mr. Mason and I would like to go and arrest Lord Cavendish of Norshire. Mr. Mason is already seconded to ODIN UK, as am I..." The prime minister glanced at Sir John, who nodded once. Before the prime minister could answer Gallin added, "It is a highly volatile situation. Lord Canvendish's reactions might be unpredictable, and I would suggest the arrest be handled by two high-ranking agents with lots of field experience." Then she added, with a face that made hard and ruthless look like Bambi, "People could get killed."

The PM held her eye a moment, then nodded. "Yes, I understand and I agree."

Sir John said, "I'll see you downstairs in five minutes," and as we reached the door the PM said, "Captain Gallin?"

We stopped and turned. Gallin said, "Yes, Prime Minister—"

"Liaise with Sir John at every step. If you need backup or support, ask for it. Do *not* cock this up."

"Understood, Prime Minister."

Out in the corridor Sir John stopped me. "It's done," he

said, frowning. "But when I spoke to the director of the Secret Service, she said they already had preparations in hand. They were just waiting on the documents."

I didn't have time to think about it then.

———

Slightly over three and a half thousand miles away, in Washington DC, it was just after six PM. Senator Peter Davis, Republican, was collecting his files to work on at home that weekend. He was a member of the House Committee on Exotic Technologies and had some research to do before the following Monday. The door to his office opened without warning and he looked up, annoyed.

"Don't we knock anymore, Hoffstadder...?" he snapped, but trailed off when he saw it was not Hoffstadder who had entered, but four men in suits who had the unmistakable look of Secret Service about them. They had the crew cuts, the wires in their ears and the shades, and though two of them were clearly Latinos and two were not, still they managed to look like clones. One of them, who managed to put across by his demeanor that he was in charge, said, "Hoffstadder had to go leave early, Senator Davis. We are instructed to inform you, sir, that we have gone code red. For your own safety, Senator, we will drive you to your country estate at Linville."

He faltered. "My wife, my kids..."

"They are waiting for you at Linville, sir."

He gestured at his attaché case. "The House Committee..."

"It's been suspended, sir. I would advise you to come

with us without delay, Senator. For your own safety. We'll have you under strict surveillance twenty-four seven, sir." He reached out. "I'll take your briefcase for you, Senator."

Senator Peter Davis handed over the case and went with the Secret Service men.

———

In Austin, Texas, it was five PM. Mitch "Sandy" Rock had finished his rib-eye at Vince Young's Steakhouse on San Jacinto Boulevard and, having drained the last of his 2017 Botanica Pinot Noir from Willamette Valley in Oregon, was contemplating a double Jim Beam on the rocks before taking Mandy and Mary-Sue back to his ranch for a little snowstorm.

He called the waiter and ordered his whiskey and a little more champagne, "for the little ladies."

They did some synchronized giggling and he said, "Let me ask you ladies something. You ever think you might see a snowstorm in Texas?"

They smiled with delighted astonishment. The joke was old but he never tired of telling it.

"You come back to my Rancho Sandy Rock with me, and I am going to show you a bli-zzard!" They laughed delightedly. "Best thing," he told them, "all that snow, and we can still strip naked and get in the pool!"

They leaned against each other, laughing, and behind them he saw the door open. Two men came in. One was in his thirties, short hair and an immaculate gray suit which was off the peg but still expensive. His pal was older, in his forties, well groomed but with a face like raw concrete. He approached the table smiling and pulled up a chair.

"Hello, Mitch."

Mitch was not happy and had a bad feeling in his belly. "I don't recall inviting you to sit down."

"Oh, that's OK," the man said, still smiling, "my name is Colonel Jan Haas. I am with the Secret Service. You ladies can leave now. The party is over."

Mitch's voice began to rise. "Hey, not you, just wait a minute, pal!" The girls scrambled, got to their feet and left on tottering feet. He turned to the colonel. "What the hell! Do you know who I am?"

The colonel leaned forward with narrowed eyes. "Oh, yes, Mitch, I know exactly who you are. You make intelligent guidance systems for missiles, and you just signed a cooperation agreement with Nano Cyber-Systems to develop the next generation of Armageddon AI rockets for your parent company, The Foundation for Computer and Cybernetic Information Technology."

Mitch frowned. "So...?"

"So we have gone Code Red, Mitch, and you can come with us for your own protection, to Rancho Sandy Rock, where we will protect you twenty-four seven until the code red is past, or I can shoot your treacherous ass right here in the restaurant. I am authorized to do that, and believe me, all I need is an excuse."

———

In Corey Hall, in Berkley, it was three in the afternoon. Professor Jon Bertrand was in his office overlooking Hearst

Avenue. He had always been a deeply intuitive man, but over the years he had learned to set his intuition aside, so that his intellect could work freely. So now, as he watched the gray Audi turn into the multi-story parking garage across the road, his intuition told him all was not well—all was very far from well. But while his intuition told him that, his intellect continued to ponder the roll of Dimethyltryptamine in forming the human experience of reality.

"The map," he quoted from Alfred Korzybski, "is not the territory."

He watched the two men in gray suits cross the road, headed for the building, and returned to his desk, piled high with papers and books, in an apparent tower of chaos.

"It mediates reality," he said and dropped into his chair, swiveling it to face the door, "but does it *create* reality, or just draw a map? Do we hallucinate reality into existence, or does the DMT filter *out* reality and leave just..."

There was a knock at the door. For a moment reality weighed heavily on his brow and he frowned.

"Come!" he said.

The door opened and the two men in gray stepped in. "Professor Bertrand?"

"Yes," he said.

"Sir, we have a code red..."

He sagged slightly but smiled a little ruefully. "It's over, isn't it?"

"Yes, sir. You'll have to come with us."

"Where are we going?"

"To Virginia, sir. To Langley. They'll come and collect your papers."

He nodded. He was not unduly alarmed. If the past

century had taught him anything, it had taught him that a willing scientist would always be on the map somewhere.

And all across the USA, and all across the UK, scientists, industrialists, financiers and politicians, one by one, were quietly taken into custody for their own protection.

At the White House the military chiefs of staff were summoned for an emergency meeting at the Oval Office. On being admitted to the office they found that the president and the vice president were not present. They had been flown to Camp David. In their place they found the director of the Secret Service standing legs akimbo in front of the president's desk, and dotted around the room six agents, each with his weapon drawn.

"Gentlemen," she said, with a smile as thin as dangerous ice, "the president would like to see you all at Camp David. We have a code red, and for your own protection I would request you surrender your weapons to my agents, and they will be returned to you upon your return." They did and said nothing, but simply stared at her. "Alternatively," she added, "we can shoot you right here."

# NINETEEN

NORSHIRE DOES NOT EXIST. IT WAS LONG AGO absorbed into Yorkshire.

Shires, in old English, "*scir,*" were areas pretty much like our counties in the USA, overseen and administered by a sheriff. The idea was that the sheriff, elected by the populace, would mediate between the Lord of the Manor and the peasants. There are lots of shires in England: Yorkshire, Lancashire, Shropshire, Wiltshire, the list goes on... but Norshire, which must once have belonged to Danish Vikings —Norse Shire—the home of the Marquis of Cavendish, no longer exists because it was absorbed into the shire of York.

All that was left of it now were traces, like the village of Goathland, Whitby and the North Yorkshire Moors National Park. None of which we saw as we thundered over the area in the RAF A109SP headed for RAF Flyingdales, a radar station near the coast and just seven miles from Lord Cavendish's ancestral home.

The Home Secretary had also insisted on sending in

ahead of us a couple of SAS squads. The eight men—enough to subdue a small country—had been dropped on the moors by chopper and had apparently surrounded the manor house. They would, according to the minister, "... keep an eye on things and make sure the whole operation was carried out discretely and without interruption."

Like I said, you have to love the Brits.

By the time we touched down at Flyingdales it was gone midnight. The base was floodlit, but completely empty, aside from one Jeep which stood at the edge of the helipad, and a captain leaning against the hood.

We thanked the pilot, ducked through the downwash and approached the RAF officer. He smiled and offered his hand.

"Good morning. I'm not here. Please don't bother telling me your names." He handed me an old-fashioned car key with a fob. "It's an old Rover 75. It's parked over by the gate. Two-minute walk in that direction. Don't bother pressing the buttons on the fob. You'll have to do it manually."

He gave a smart salute, climbed in his Jeep and drove away. We set off at a quick walk through the dark toward the road. We soon came to the elegant old burgundy Rover, parked beside the gate. I got behind the wheel and Gallin climbed in beside me. While I fired up the V6 engine she checked her weapon for the third time.

"You're nervous?" I said, as I pulled away.

"He's a Lord of the Real," she said. "His family have been lords for nearly a thousand years. It may not mean much to you, being a Yank, but to us it's almost sacrilegious."

We drove in silence for a while, headed north through pitch-black moorland. Eventually I said, "So are you English or Israeli? I'm not talking about your passports. I'm talking about you."

She studied me for a while. Then said, "There were Jews in England a thousand years before Israel was founded. We came over with William the Conqueror in 1066. We've been here as long as the Normans. And being English does not take away one jot from being Israeli."

I nodded and we fell silent again. After a while I asked, "So this guy's family have been lords in the north of England for as long as there have been Jews in England."

"Pretty much, yeah. Don't ask me why that matters, but it does." Then she surprised me by adding, "Our ancient liberties, our freedoms, our stand against tyranny, that ancient battle of the free individual against the oppressive state, all of that is rooted in tradition, in history."

I was going to tell her I agreed, but she cut me short.

"Did you know that in 1215, over eight hundred years ago, an assembly of barons, the first green shoots of Parliament, forced King John to sign the Magna Carta granting, and I quote, 'to all freemen of our kingdom' the rights and liberties described in the charter? The charter was used in at the end of the century to stop Edward I from imposing harsh taxes to finance his war against the French, and as a result it was entered into the Statutes of England. That makes it a foundation stone of English law, and of Western parliamentary democracy."

I opened my mouth but she cut me short again. "So much so," she said, wagging her finger at me, "that of the four 1297 originals that remain, one was purchased by David

Rubenstein and loaned to the American people, to be displayed in the National Archive, as a reminder that your inalienable rights are rooted in your ancient liberties, which in turn are rooted in ancient Nordic culture."

"Gallin?"

"What?"

"Aside from the fact that I do know, why are you telling me all this?"

She sighed. "Because it was what Saul Epstein was all about. And it is the reason we are on our way to Lord Cavendish's ancestral home. Who was it who said to us that the power of the people must be focused through the lens of the Crown...?"

"Sir John, at the Italian Gardens, where Henry VIII used to hunt."

"Saul was the rebellious 'people,' refusing to lie down and be subjugated. Lord Cavendish represents the Crown, refusing to recognize the source of its power..." She trailed off.

"And you," I asked softly. "What are you?"

"Me?" She gave a small, humorless snort. "I am Nemesis, she who brings what is due."

Just after Goathland we turned left onto Stape Road, a narrow track barely wide enough for two vehicles. It ran straight across open moorland for three miles and the came to an intersection. Here I pulled over onto the grass verge and climbed out. I wondered absently if I was being watched by an SAS sniper, and decided I probably was.

There was a wooden stake, like the ones you used to see in children's fairy tales, and it had three arrows nailed to the top of the post. One pointed back the way we'd come and said "Goath Land" as two words, the other pointed on the way we were going and said "Stape," and the third pointed to a dirt track that wound into the moor, and said "Norshire Manor."

We had to haul open a rough gate made of steel tubing suspended at one end from a heavy wooden stake. Then we followed the track, lurching and bumping over potholes and loose rocks for three miles across what must have been stunning landscapes of heather and rolling hills, but was completely invisible to us in the darkness of the night.

After ten or fifteen minutes we finally saw the silhouette of the manor house rise against the paler darkness of the horizon. I killed the lights and followed the ribbon of the dirt track toward the black, spired and chimneyed hulk of the house. Soon we became aware that the house itself was surrounded by a redbrick wall some ten feet high, and the track we were following led to a large iron gate in that wall.

I stopped the car and climbed out, wondering whether to use a 9mm key to open the lock. But a brief inspection showed me the gate was not locked. There was a large, iron bolt with a massive padlock, but it had been pulled back and the gate yielded easily and silently to my push.

I climbed back in and the drive led us now through woodland and well-kept gardens to the vast, rambling house. It was dark, but for one, ground-floor window which issued a pale, amber glow from behind half-closed drapes.

We climbed out of the car and, far away in the east, over the North Sea, sheet lightning illuminated the sky, in silence. By contrast our steps as we crossed the gravel sounded loud in the night.

There was a brass chain hanging beside the door, but we

didn't need to pull it. The door opened as we approached, and an old-world butler, in a black coat and striped gray pants, bowed to us and made an inquiry of his face.

"I am Alex Mason, and this is Captain Aila Gallin. We are here to see Lord Cavendish." As an afterthought I added, "I am not sure if we are expected."

"M'Lord is expecting you. He is in his study, if you'll follow me."

We followed him, across ancient wooden floors strewn with rugs, to an oak door set in a Tudor arch that actually was a Tudor arch, where he knocked, opened the door and stepped inside.

"Mr. Mason, M'Lord, and Captain Gallin."

I didn't hear the answer, but the butler stepped back and allowed us to enter.

I don't know what I expected, but it wasn't this. The study was not vast, but it was a comfortable size. He had an oak desk that had probably belonged to all his ancestors for the past eight hundred years. It was chipped and scratched, and hadn't been polished for far too long.

It stood beside a giant, Tudor fireplace where great logs were burning, and the light from the flames wavered and reflected on his desk, on the thousands of books that lined the room and spilled from the bookcases, on his cracked, scuffed leather armchairs and on his large, aquiline head, where he stood stooped, looking down at the flames.

The door closed behind us and he spoke loudly to the flames.

"You're impertinent," he said. "Of course anything goes these days." He turned and looked first at me and then at

Gallin, with severe, aquiline eyes as pale as blue ice. "But that does not change the fact. You are impertinent."

"I apologize," I said, "but we have to do what we have to do."

"Tautology," he replied with no particular emphasis. "Anesthetic for the brain." He had his hands deep in his corduroy pants pockets, and a gray cardigan which looked like it had been knitted by his granddaughter. His great domed head was bald, but for an unruly mass of white curls at the back of his head.

"I will not die in prison," he said.

"No—"

He glanced at me. "Doesn't it strike you as odd, Mr. Mason, that throughout history, the man tasked with the execution of another is the one who knows least about his crimes?"

"I had never really thought about it."

"Of course you hadn't." And after a moment he sighed and added, "You may as well sit, I am not going to resist arrest."

He had two ancient leather wingchairs facing his desk. We sat in them and he turned to face us.

"I am the single most powerful man on the planet," he said unexpectedly. "Bill Gates, Elon Musk, that appalling Zuckerberg—jumped-up princelings. The power, the true temporal power on this orb belongs to a small family." He smiled and then chuckled. "Washington, the War of Independence, the Federal Reserve—" He threw back his head and laughed out loud. "Do you know who owns the Federal Reserve?" Neither of us answered. He didn't expect us to.

"Whoever owns the Federal Reserve owns America, that much you do know."

He took a deep, heavy breath. "There are two kinds of people in this world." He looked at Gallin and smiled. "There is the vast majority, rushing mindlessly toward nine billion in number, and they are the hive. They don't even know they exist. The kindest thing one can say about them is that they are the must from which spirit is distilled. More accurately, they are the scum from which life springs."

Gallin asked, "And the others?"

"The others are gods."

I laughed and he smiled at me. "Gods?"

"You are as ignorant as an ant," he said, still smiling. "Brought up in the Judeo-Christian tradition, you think of gods as absolute beings, shapeless, omnipotent, omnipresent. But the gods are simply powerful beyond human understanding. And their power comes from the simple, visceral knowledge that we exist. That we are unique, divine, indestructible and as powerful as our ability to believe." His smile became almost benign. "I am a god. Captain Gallin, Mr. Mason, you are drones whose place is in the hive. You can never imprison me, and you can never destroy me."

I was getting bored and I sighed. "Lord Cavendish, returning briefly to the planet Earth, you are talking about your immense power and how you are indestructible, but here we are. Your coups failed and all your co-conspirators are under arrest. So, forgive me for saying so, but there is something wrong with your picture."

He chuckled and ran his hand over his desk.

"There was no planned coup, Mr. Mason. That isn't due for another five to ten years, with the cull."

Gallin frowned. "Wait, *what?*"

"It is not a fixed date. When the population reaches about nine billion, then we will institute the cull. What your generation would call a reboot. But that is not due for another ten years, roughly."

I shook my head. "But Saul's research..."

"Yes, indeed, there are some brilliant scientists playing with nano-technology and genetics. Many of them work for us, and some of them fantasize about some kind of *Star Trek* future populated by perfect, cybernetically enhanced humans. But that was never part of our plan, and certainly not part of FUCCIT's brief." He laughed again. "Why would we want the drones to be able to compete with us? Why would we enhance their capabilities? You are fine just as you are: stupid enough to control, clever enough to perform quite complex tasks."

I scratched my head. "But then, the purpose of FUCCIT? The conspiracy Saul uncovered...?"

He leaned forward with his elbows on the table and his hands clasped in front of him. His eyes were like two pale blue lasers.

"Alex, there is one, and only one, source of temporal power. You know this, you have heard it before. That source of power is *violence*. We, the gods, must have absolute control of the means of violence on this planet. So we invest a lot of time, effort, research and money into perfecting the means of inflicting violence. That is to say, we select the best of the drones to do that for us. And all the while we keep the drones at war with each other, so that we can keep applying that violence. Because *violence is the only source of true temporal power*. Do you understand?"

"And that's why you didn't kill him."

"We had no reason at all to kill Saul."

Gallin said, "Wait, what?"

Cavendish shrugged. "I rarely interfere with the drones. But in this case I wish I had. Somebody killed Saul, for reasons best known to themselves, and triggered panic reactions among the more well-informed and secretive organizations like ODIN, because they thought the so-called military-industrial complex was about to execute a coup. As I say, that will happen, but not for another ten years at least.

"So when ODIN went into a flat spin and started calling in agents to investigate, FUCCIT started to panic, along with numerous leaders of the deep state, and Richard Chen —a very able man whom you beheaded, Mr. Mason—went into action to stop you from stopping a coup that was never planned in the first place."

Gallin was staring from me to Cavendish, shaking her head. "So the whole damned thing..."

He shrugged his bony shoulders. "It was a storm in a teacup that was never planned or intended. Because somebody shot Saul, and everybody panicked." He leaned forward again. "Captain Gallin, let me see if I can explain this to you in a way that you will understand. This planet..." He looked up at his polished wooden rafters. "Think of this planet as hell. In order to survive we must eat each other, pain in this three-dimensional world is inescapable, the only sure outcome is death, this is hell in all its nine, inglorious levels. Knowing that provides us with a choice: to serve or to rule. Well—" He gave a small laugh. "Better to rule in Hell, than to serve in Heaven. So, that raises the question, how do we rule in Hell?"

"Violence."

"There, you see? Violence, the only true source of power. We own the means of violence, and we spend our time fostering conflict at every level of human society, partly to keep the violence going, and partly so they are far too busy hating each other's hives, to even notice that we exist."

She shook her head. "Who are you? You talk about 'we.' Who? Who *are* you?"

"The gods, captain Gallin. The gods."

I was gripped by a sudden certainty. I stood and pulled the P226 from under my arm and pointed it at his head. I said, "Gods, but mortal gods."

He didn't even blink. The slug slammed his head back against the headrest and a moment later his blood oozed down onto his shoulders. Gallin looked at me and we made our way out of the office toward the front door.

It burst open before we got there and four men in black, wearing balaclavas and carrying Carbines, ran past us toward the office. We descended the stairs toward the Rover.

# TWENTY

IT WAS STILL RAINING. THE DROPS PATTERED ON Sir John's window, like they had almost given up trying to get in, but not quite. He had a small fire burning in the grate, and a decanter of whiskey on the desk which we were sipping.

"Well, I'm sorry it's been a bit rough." He said it like he'd invited us to a cocktail party where one of the guests had got drunk. "Don't think any of us expected things to get quite that wild, eh?"

"So Lord Cavendish was crazy?" It was Gallin, sounding skeptical.

"Apparently he had insipient dementia which had caused a psychotic break. His wife provided us with the medical diagnosis. They'd kept it from his various boards of directors, of course. Very improper, but there we are. Gave us all a bit of a scare."

"And Saul?"

"Well, to some extent it was as Lord Cavendish said. Saul's murder triggered a panic reaction at ODIN, not to mention a raft of other security organizations, which led to a kind of chain reaction. Of course, Lord C, being already a bit batty, had employed that appalling Richard Chen as director of security at The Foundation for Computer whatsit—"

"FUCCIT—"

"Quite so, and he went off the deep end and decided he had to eliminate you, so the whole thing escalated out of hand."

I asked, "And he murdered Saul, or had him killed."

"Apparently. That is what the documents we have seized seem to suggest."

"But if the whole thing was triggered by Saul's death..."

"That's to say," he interrupted me, "Chen must have got wind of Saul's documentary, and taken it upon himself to eliminate him, thus triggering the whole fiasco."

Gallin was shaking her head. "But what of the deep state, democracy, all the arrests, the coup..."

Sir John smiled. "Let's see how many more years of uneasy truce we can squeeze out of them."


Out in the street I hailed a black cab. We climbed in and I told the cabby, "Kensington Church Street, the Churchill Pub."

"What's this?" Gallin was frowning at me. "We need to go back to my place and pack. Our flight takes off in four hours."

I nodded. "I know. It won't take long. There is one place in Saul's apartment we didn't check."

"Check for what? We know what happened to the documentary. He gave it to Sir John for safekeeping."

"Yeah, I know..." I trailed off, looking out at the bleak drizzle. "I was thinking about his autobiography. What happened to that? And Richard Chen. You know, Lord Cavendish had obviously filled his head with all that god crap, he'd begun to believe he was a god himself, but the fact is he made a lot of mistakes. He was not real smart, and I wouldn't mind having one last look around. If he killed Saul, he left some trace behind."

She didn't answer, and after a short while we pulled up outside the Churchill, I paid the cabby and we strolled down through the drizzle to Saul's apartment.

Gallin let us in with her magic key and I left the front door open as we walked into the living room. It was just as we had left it. Only, it had acquired a slightly musty, damp smell. I stood staring around, a little aimlessly, while Gallin watched me and tried to repress her impatience. Finally she snapped,

"Mason, you and I both know that it is not possible for Chen to have killed Saul. Saul was killed by somebody from his intimate circle. They are covering for somebody. If you ask me, my money is on his wife."

I smiled at her. "Hell hath no fury like a woman scorned." I shrugged. ".45 is a hell of a cannon for a lady. Besides, she loved him. You don't shoot a guy you love in the face with a .45, Gallin. Even you wouldn't do that. I don't think it's a coverup, Gallin. I think they just want it to go away."

"Would you mind telling me what we are doing here, then?"

Out on the landing the elevator hissed to a halt and the automatic doors clattered open. A moment later Simon stood in the doorway. He didn't look happy.

"Hello, Simon."

"You can't keep coming here and letting yourselves in."

"We are going to have to, until we find his autobiography."

"You can't."

"Why not?"

"Because it's not here."

"Who did you sell it to?"

"It's mine. He gave it to me."

Gallin frowned. "He gave it to you?"

"And I can prove it. He dedicated it to me. It said, 'To Simon Hamilton, who opened my eyes to the beauty of simplicity.'"

I shook my head and made a "don't care" face. "I am not going to argue with that, Simon. I figure you were the best friend Saul had. But here's the thing. If you sell that manuscript without it going through the proper probate channels, they will come, they will take the book away from the publisher and they will take all your money away. You see, you can have the book and the money, but you have to do it properly."

"You are trying to trick me."

I laughed. "I don't need to trick you, Simon, I just need to call the cops. I'm trying to help you. Have you sold it already?"

He shook his head. "My agent is still negotiating."

"Good, so we need to make sure that it goes to probate. You have it in your apartment downstairs?"

He nodded. His eyes were wary, and turning wild. He was scared. I took out my phone and called Sir John. When he answered I said, "Joanna? Listen, this is Alex. We have a little situation we need to iron out. Regarding Saul's autobiography. Yeah, he left it to Simon Hamilton, a really nice guy who lives and works in the building. He and Saul were really good friends. So, what we want to avoid is that the manuscript gets snatched back into the estate. Are you following me? So we will need probate to give that the OK."

Sir John said, "My dear chap, I have no idea what you are talking about. The janitor...?"

"Exactly, now hang on, I'll ask him." I turned to Simon, who seemed to have relaxed a bit, and said, "He needs to know, the revolver you used to shoot him, was that registered in the UK or did you bring it over in the diplomatic pouch with your dad?"

For a moment I thought I'd blown it. He blinked three times while he tried to process the implications of the question, but like he'd told me, under pressure he got nervous and made mistakes. After the third blink he said, "I brought it over in the diplomatic pouch."

Into the phone I said, "You got that, Joanna? Yeah, we need to clear it with probate so he can sell the manuscript," and I hung up.

He was staring at the floor. "I cocked up, didn't I?"

I shrugged and shook my head. "Why'd you kill him? He was a good man, and a good friend to you."

He squeezed his brows together, trying to understand how we could be so stupid. "For the money," he said. "He kept telling me how famous he was going to be, how his documentary was going to rock the world. I liked him at first and I wouldn't have killed him, but he'd started hugging me and touching me all the time, and talking about how close we were and I was his only real close friend. I *hate* that. I kept telling him, 'Don't touch me! I don't like touching!' but he just laughed and insisted we were close friends. So when I went home I collected the Smith and Wesson I'd bought in Arizona, and I shot him." He went quiet for a while. Then he said, "But when I went to get the documentary, it had gone. He must have given it to somebody while I was away. So I took his autobiography instead. I should get some money from that, shouldn't I?"

I felt suddenly depressed. "Yeah," I said, "once probate clears it."

HALF AN HOUR later we stood in the rain on the sidewalk and watched the red taillights of two police cars disappear toward Notting Hill Gate. Gallin punched me on the shoulder and said, "That was good. Good, clear thinking."

I shrugged. "Sir John had told us that Saul had told him he would be the first to see it when it was finished, which made sense if Sir John was his inside source. With everybody else eliminated, and the documentary no longer the motive for the killing, it left just one person: a person whom Saul treated as an intimate friend, liked to have around, had access to weapons and had shown an abiding interest in money. When Cavendish told us even they didn't know who'd killed Saul, that clinched it."

I hailed a passing cab and as we climbed in I gave the

cabby Gallin's address. As we pulled away she said, "So now we fly to DC and then Camp David? I can't believe it. What's at Camp David?"

I settled back in the seat and smiled. "Unless I am very much mistaken, there will be the president and the vice president, with their families, there will be the military chiefs of staff, the chief of the Secret Service and..."

I looked at her. She smiled uncertainly. "And...?"

"And a fat bastard who faked his own death so he could take the deep state cabal off guard while he masterminded their arrests. He'd seen them grow too big, and this was just the opportunity he needed to bring them down a notch."

"You mean...?"

"Yeah, Nero. We'll never know, but my guess is he got Sir John to infiltrate FUCCIT and feed intel to Saul. When Saul died, and both sides panicked, he saw the opportunity. If he was murdered the White House and the Secret Service would fear a coup and be ready to act on the information we gave them."

"Son of a bitch. You sure?"

I nodded. "Remember what Sir John said when we were at Number 10? He said the chief of the Secret Service had told him they already had everything in place. They were just waiting for the documents. The deep state is going to be a lot weaker after this, and Congress might just be able to impose some accountability on the military-industrial complex. We'll see."

As we rolled down Holland Park Avenue toward Gallin's house my cell rang. I glanced at the screen and answered.

"Hey, Lovelock. We're just—"

"Alex, it is I, Nero. I am sick of politicians. You can meet the president at some later date, next week. I shall be at home, bring Captain Gallin and we shall dine there, I was thinking oysters, and perhaps a rack of lamb. Or do you favor beef? But beef is too strong after oysters, perhaps..."

I looked at Gallin. She smiled and reached out with one finger and wiped the tear from my cheek.

**Don't miss ALL THE KING'S MEN. The riveting sequel in the Alex Mason Thriller series.**

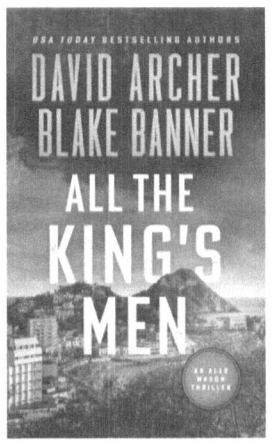

Scan the QR code below to purchase ALL THE KING'S MEN.

Or go to: righthouse.com/all-the-kings-men

*NOTE: flip to the very end to read an exclusive sneak peak...*

# DON'T MISS ANYTHING!

If you want to stay up to date on all new releases in this series, with these authors, or with any of our new deals, you can do so by joining our newsletters below.

In addition, you will immediately gain access to our entire *Right House VIP Library,* which currently includes *ORIGINS*—a full length prequel novel to *ODIN.*

righthouse.com/email

*(Easy to unsubscribe. No spam. Ever.)*

# ALSO BY DAVID ARCHER

Up to date books can be found at:
www.righthouse.com/david-archer

## ROGUE THRILLERS
Gates of Hell (Book 1)
Hell's Fury (Book 2)

## JACOB HUNTER THRILLERS
The Kyiv File (Book 1)
The Bogota File (Book 2)

## PETER BLACK THRILLERS
Burden of the Assassin (Book 1)
The Man Without A Face (Book 2)
Unpunished Deeds (Book 3)
Hunter Killer (Book 4)
Silent Shadows (Book 5)
The Last Run (Book 6)
Dark Corners (Book 7)
Ghost Operative (Book 8)

## ALEX MASON THRILLERS
Odin (Book 1)
Ice Cold Spy (Book 2)
Mason's Law (Book 3)
Assets and Liabilities (Book 4)
Russian Roulette (Book 5)

Executive Order (Book 6)
Dead Man Talking (Book 7)
All The King's Men (Book 8)
Flashpoint (Book 9)
Brotherhood of the Goat (Book 10)
Dead Hot (Book 11)
Blood on Megiddo (Book 12)
Son of Hell (Book 13)

## NOAH WOLF THRILLERS

Code Name Camelot (Book 1)
Lone Wolf (Book 2)
In Sheep's Clothing (Book 3)
Hit for Hire (Book 4)
The Wolf's Bite (Book 5)
Black Sheep (Book 6)
Balance of Power (Book 7)
Time to Hunt (Book 8)
Red Square (Book 9)
Highest Order (Book 10)
Edge of Anarchy (Book 11)
Unknown Evil (Book 12)
Black Harvest (Book 13)
World Order (Book 14)
Caged Animal (Book 15)
Deep Allegiance (Book 16)
Pack Leader (Book 17)
High Treason (Book 18)
A Wolf Among Men (Book 19)
Rogue Intelligence (Book 20)
Alpha (Book 21)

Rogue Wolf (Book 22)
Shadows of Allegiance (Book 23)
In the Grip of Darkness (Book 24)

## SAM PRICHARD MYSTERIES
The Grave Man (Book 1)
Death Sung Softly (Book 2)
Love and War (Book 3)
Framed (Book 4)
The Kill List (Book 5)
Drifter: Part One (Book 6)
Drifter: Part Two (Book 7)
Drifter: Part Three (Book 8)
The Last Song (Book 9)
Ghost (Book 10)
Hidden Agenda (Book 11)

## SAM AND INDIE MYSTERIES
Aces and Eights (Book 1)
Fact or Fiction (Book 2)
Close to Home (Book 3)
Brave New World (Book 4)
Innocent Conspiracy (Book 5)
Unfinished Business (Book 6)
Live Bait (Book 7)
Alter Ego (Book 8)
More Than It Seems (Book 9)
Moving On (Book 10)
Worst Nightmare (Book 11)
Chasing Ghosts (Book 12)
Serial Superstition (Book 13)

**CHANCE REDDICK THRILLERS**
Innocent Injustice (Book 1)
Angel of Justice (Book 2)
High Stakes Hunting (Book 3)
Personal Asset (Book 4)

**CASSIE MCGRAW MYSTERIES**
What Lies Beneath (Book 1)
Can't Fight Fate (Book 2)
One Last Game (Book 3)
Never Really Gone (Book 4)

# ALSO BY BLAKE BANNER

Up to date books can be found at:
www.righthouse.com/blake-banner

### ROGUE THRILLERS
Gates of Hell (Book 1)
Hell's Fury (Book 2)

### ALEX MASON THRILLERS
Odin (Book 1)
Ice Cold Spy (Book 2)
Mason's Law (Book 3)
Assets and Liabilities (Book 4)
Russian Roulette (Book 5)
Executive Order (Book 6)
Dead Man Talking (Book 7)
All The King's Men (Book 8)
Flashpoint (Book 9)
Brotherhood of the Goat (Book 10)
Dead Hot (Book 11)
Blood on Megiddo (Book 12)
Son of Hell (Book 13)

### HARRY BAUER THRILLER SERIES
Dead of Night (Book 1)
Dying Breath (Book 2)
The Einstaat Brief (Book 3)

Quantum Kill (Book 4)
Immortal Hate (Book 5)
The Silent Blade (Book 6)
LA: Wild Justice (Book 7)
Breath of Hell (Book 8)
Invisible Evil (Book 9)
The Shadow of Ukupacha (Book 10)
Sweet Razor Cut (Book 11)
Blood of the Innocent (Book 12)
Blood on Balthazar (Book 13)
Simple Kill (Book 14)
Riding The Devil (Book 15)
The Unavenged (Book 16)
The Devil's Vengeance (Book 17)
Bloody Retribution (Book 18)
Rogue Kill (Book 19)
Blood for Blood (Book 20)

## DEAD COLD MYSTERY SERIES
An Ace and a Pair (Book 1)
Two Bare Arms (Book 2)
Garden of the Damned (Book 3)
Let Us Prey (Book 4)
The Sins of the Father (Book 5)
Strange and Sinister Path (Book 6)
The Heart to Kill (Book 7)
Unnatural Murder (Book 8)
Fire from Heaven (Book 9)
To Kill Upon A Kiss (Book 10)
Murder Most Scottish (Book 11)

The Butcher of Whitechapel (Book 12)
Little Dead Riding Hood (Book 13)
Trick or Treat (Book 14)
Blood Into Wine (Book 15)
Jack In The Box (Book 16)
The Fall Moon (Book 17)
Blood In Babylon (Book 18)
Death In Dexter (Book 19)
Mustang Sally (Book 20)
A Christmas Killing (Book 21)
Mommy's Little Killer (Book 22)
Bleed Out (Book 23)
Dead and Buried (Book 24)
In Hot Blood (Book 25)
Fallen Angels (Book 26)
Knife Edge (Book 27)
Along Came A Spider (Book 28)
Cold Blood (Book 29)
Curtain Call (Book 30)

## THE OMEGA SERIES
Dawn of the Hunter (Book 1)
Double Edged Blade (Book 2)
The Storm (Book 3)
The Hand of War (Book 4)
A Harvest of Blood (Book 5)
To Rule in Hell (Book 6)
Kill: One (Book 7)
Powder Burn (Book 8)
Kill: Two (Book 9)
Unleashed (Book 10)

# ABOUT US

Right House is an independent publisher created by authors for readers. We specialize in Action, Thriller, Mystery, and Crime novels.

If you enjoyed this novel, then there is a good chance you will like what else we have to offer! Please stay up to date by using any of the links below.

Join our mailing lists to stay up to date -->
righthouse.com/email
Visit our website --> righthouse.com
Contact us --> contact@righthouse.com

 facebook.com/righthousebooks
 x.com/righthousebooks
 instagram.com/righthousebooks

# EXCLUSIVE SNEAK PEAK OF...

**ALL THE KING'S MEN**

# PROLOGUE

Colonel Ian Cameron, retired, late of the Central Intelligence Agency, looked out at his audience and smiled with the confidence of a man who has faced violent death so many times he has forgotten how to be scared.

"This book," he said, "is the story of my life," he paused a moment to give a brief, ironic laugh, "or at least that part of it, after I was eighteen, when the illegal things I did had the blessing of the Federal Government." There was laughter around the brightly lit room. "That made life a lot easier, I can tell you. Those first eighteen years will have to remain my secret. Let me just say that the midwife's first word when I was born was 'Oops!' and my mother's first six words to the midwife were, 'What is the policy on returns?'"

There was more laughter, almost an uproar. They'd had enough wine and brandy to laugh at anything, and the colonel's delivery was good.

"I know," he went on. "I could have been a stand-up comedian, but the comedians make this stuff up." He paused and became serious. "But what I'm doing is telling you the truth." The laughter died away. "When I was eighteen I joined Delta Force, which you are told doesn't actually exist. I can tell you it does. It is very real. When I joined them I had the moral and ethical standards of a Mexican second-hand car dealer." He smiled and shook his head. "I'll tell you! I once had a meeting with Bill Clinton, you can read all about it in the book, and he left the meeting in tears, sobbing, 'Lord forgive me, I have seen the error of my ways!' Seriously, he went and joined the Quakers after that. I met Hillary and she kept calling me Lord."

They were in stitches again, and one guy was slapping his thigh.

"I'm kidding, that never happened. Not like that, anyway. But from Delta I was recruited into the Central Intelligence Agency. They told me they'd recruited me because, in the psych evaluation I had scored zero in moral inhibitions. They said there was no moral—or immoral—place I was not prepared to go. And I gotta tell you, back then, that was true. There are people like that. I have met them. The Mexican cartels are made up of people like that. But what is worrying, my friends, is when Western security agencies, those agencies charged with protecting democracy and our Federal Government, recruit you *because* you are like that. I should have been in a mental institution, or better still on Death Row. But they couldn't do that to me because in the beginning I was too valuable to them, and later because everything I had done I had done with their blessing. And besides."

He looked around the room at the faces, wide-eyed and wondering, warm with admiration.

"Don't ask me how it happened. I don't really know myself. But you look into enough pleading eyes, you see enough orphaned children, enough destroyed families, and something begins to happen inside of you. I am not just talking about the *hundreds of thousands* of people murdered and orphaned in Mexico, so that those bastards can become billionaires. I am talking also about driving through DC, Philly or Chicago, or any other city in the USA, and seeing the junkies, the junkies' children, the wasted lives, the hollow, uncomprehending eyes too wasted even to plead. I am talking about seeing that and knowing that you enabled it. That you made it possible."

He paused a long time, leaning on the lectern and staring at the floor.

"Something," he said and looked out at his audience again, "something inside you begins to stir and wake up, and you know that somehow it is wrong, and you have to stop. I don't know if there's a god, and if there is I don't know if it is a monster or a god of love and forgiveness. And I have no idea how to define good and evil. But what I can tell you is that I know in my bones that what I did for all those years was wrong, and now, somehow, I have to atone. So fifty percent of the proceeds of this book will go to setting up a foundation to help children who are the victims of parents who abuse or trade in drugs." There was applause. When it died down he added, jabbing his finger toward the cardboard display by the door, "But equally important is that, if I must atone, the bastards who recruited me, who shielded me and enabled me to do the things I did, must atone also. There are pillars of society in this country who have grown rich—fabulously rich—on the pain and suffering of millions of men, women and children from Chiapas and Yucatan to Chihuahua and Sonora. This book will be published in a month. Advanced sales are already through the roof. Good! Because when this book hits the stands, my friends, heads are going to roll from the White House to the National Palace in Mexico City! The time has come for a lot of people to take responsibility for what they have done. I am the first, but believe me, I am not the last!"

The room erupted in applause. People got to their feet, clapping, whistling and shouting. From a table just in front of the lectern, Araminta Whitley, his publisher, stood and came to join him. They hugged, taking care to keep looking out at the audience, where cameras were flashing, and after a moment she approached the lectern and the microphone.

"Dear friends...dear friends..." The applause and the noise gradually died down and people returned to their seats. "Dear friends," she said again, "we are today in the presence of a truly remarkable man who, raised in an environment of violence, crime and cruelty, set out to take control—to own his own life. And though he had to go through hell to get there, he eventually found his own humanity and is now ready and willing—having faced his own monsters—to face the monsters in Washington DC and elsewhere, and bring them to account. This book, when it hits the stands in one month, will send seismic shock waves through the Capitol and the White House *and* the Pentagon. Make a note of the title and if you haven't done so already, order your copy now! *Sex Drugs and Rock 'n' Roll at the White House!*"

They hugged again, this time more intimately, among the sudden noise of people breaking into conversation, rising from their tables or calling for drinks. As he released her he said, "In my day they'd have put out a hit on me. These days I don't think they'd dare."

She laughed. "I hope you're right. I want at least another two books out of you. And I *want* that autobiography!"

He grinned. "I plead the fifth. I'll call you tomorrow. Maybe we can have lunch."

She wagged a finger at him. "If I haven't heard from you by eleven, I'll call you!"

He held both her hands and squeezed them, then turned and moved through the crowd, stopping here and there to exchange a few words, kiss the ladies and slap the men's shoulders.

Finally he made it to the hotel lobby, where he paused to pull a pack of Camels from his tuxedo pocket and poke one in his mouth. He flipped open an old, battered Zippo, leaned into the flame and headed toward the door. On his way he grinned at the worried-looking concierge. "Lifetime of breaking rules, I'm not going to stop now, right? Don't worry, I'm on my way out."

Outside, at the bottom of the red-carpeted steps he paused beside the grotesque gilt lamp, thrust his right hand in his trouser pocket and took a drag. He inhaled the smoke deep into his lungs, then raised his chin to blow a long stream of smoke into the night air.

Across the road an old guy with a long beard and a hat was leaning against the wall, watching him. The trees of Central Park towered above him, and beside him he had a small dog in an ancient pram. Colonel Ian Cameron touched his forehead with two fingers in a salute. Choices, he told himself, it's all about the choices you make.

He turned right, and though it was cold, he strolled. He

liked New York. He liked New York at night. He liked the lights and the people and the skyscrapers that had once been futuristic and were now classical and reminiscent of Orson Welles and Scott Fitzgerald. He passed the Pulitzer Fountain, not sure where he was going, but thinking about where to stop for a nightcap.

That was when he saw the gorgeous brunette walking toward him in a hurry and smiling. She was ten feet away in a scarlet dress that was hugging her like it never wanted to let go, and a cute red pillbox on her head, when she said, "Colonel? Colonel Ian Cameron? Don't you remember me?"

He took a drag as she drew closer and said, "I feel like I ought to."

She giggled and placed a red satin-gloved hand on his chest. "There is a man behind you with a Maxim 9 pointed at your lower back. It will cripple you for life, but we'll get you to a doctor in that SUV," she pointed to a black Mercedes that had pulled up by the sidewalk with its hazards flashing, "before you die. And you'll live the rest of your life as a pathetic cripple."

She came in close and took hold of his satin lapels. "So why don't you do the smart thing and get in the back of the car, so we can talk in private?"

Two guys in suits had climbed out of the SUV and had approached them where they stood. He turned and saw she hadn't lied about the guy behind him. He figured they hadn't killed him—and he knew they could have—so they wanted something. That meant it was safer to go along than to try and fight or run. He shrugged.

"If I come along quietly, can I take you to dinner later?"

"Oh," she gave a laugh that was as funny as swimming naked in a frozen lake in Siberia, "you *really* don't want to do that."

They bundled him discretely into the Merc. A few people glanced, but he wasn't struggling and the people around him were smiling and chatting. So nobody raised the alarm. Then they were sliding the doors closed and two guys climbed in the cab, and the SUV pulled out into the traffic, nice and steady.

In the back the colonel looked at the two guys next to him, and the beautiful woman opposite. Something in her eyes made him uneasy.

"Where are we going?"

It was violent and unexpected. The guy on his right grabbed his wrist and twisted savagely while the guy on his left grabbed his head and forced him forward, so his brow was pressed on his knees. The woman pulled up his jacket and wrenched his shirt out of his pants. Then he felt a piercing, burning agony in his back.

They let him go and he sat upright, gasping. Hot rage was burning in his head, but the cannons of two Maxim 9s stopped him before he could act. The woman said, "Easy, Colonel. See this?" She showed him her cell phone. "Yes, it's my phone, but it is also a detonator. I have just injected a capsule of high explosive next to your spine. It's not enough to bring down a plane or demolish a building, but it's enough to blow your spine in half. All I have to do is dial the right number. So from this moment on, you are going to do just exactly as I say. Do you *comprende, compadre*?"

"You bitch. Where are you taking me?"

"Oh, don't worry, you'll like it," she said. "You and me

are going to Mexico. We're going to visit some old friends of yours. They will be really happy to see you again, now that you've become a famous author, an' all."

Colonel Ian Cameron sank back into the black leather seat. He had taken care not to offend or upset Ismael Zamora or Francisco Gallardo. He had spoken to them and cleared everything with them first. The rest of them at the Company, the White House and the Capitol he didn't give a damn about. But Sinaloa were his friends, his tribe. He did not want to upset them. He eyed the beautiful killer opposite him and wondered if they had sent her. If they had, by the look in her eyes, he had offended them.

And badly.

# CHAPTER 1

AT THREE MINUTES PAST ELEVEN THE NEXT morning, Araminta Whitley stood at the sixteenth-floor window of her office at Oddhouse Publishing, on the corner of 55$^{th}$ and Broadway, tapping her foot. She sighed deeply and picked up her phone. "Jamilla, get me Colonel Cameron on the phone, please."

"Will do."

She hung up and stood scanning the taxis far below. When her phone rang two minutes later she forced herself to count to four before answering.

"Yes?"

She was surprised not to hear Jamilla's voice. It was a man's, vaguely familiar.

"Araminta?"

"Yes...?"

"This is Alasdair Cameron, Ian's brother."

"Oh!" She laughed, like it was funny it should be him

and not somebody else. "I didn't recognize you. How *are* you?"

He sounded like he'd been asleep for the past fifty years and wasn't sure he wanted to wake up.

"Well, I'm a little worried, Araminta. You see, Ian said he was going to see you last night, for his book launch—"

"That's not a reason to be worried, darling."

"Um," he wasn't sure if he was supposed to laugh or not, so he did something odd with his voice, like a small cough, and went on, "that's why I'm calling you. You see, he didn't come home last night. And since he's been back to New York, he has been very particular about either coming home, or telling me where he is going to be. A security thing, or something. And you know yourself, he is very punctual, always."

She was quiet for a moment. "He lives with you?"

"We share the old family home on East 78th Street, just by the park," he added inconsequentially. "He said he'd be home around midnight, but there's no sign of him, and I can't get an answer from his phone. Do you know where he is?"

She could feel a hot bead of anxiety in her belly, but she laughed. "You know what an old scoundrel he is! He left the launch around eleven and probably went to a bar and got drunk with some gorgeous babe. I am expecting him now. We are supposed to have a meeting before lunch. I'll tell him off for you and get him to call as soon as he comes in."

"Thank you, Araminta. I *am* worried. I..." He hesitated, then gave a sigh that was very sad. "I really think he has gone too far this time."

He didn't wait for a reply. He just hung up and left her

with her phone pressed to her ear, looking at the yellow cabs far below. They were collecting and delivering their passengers, but not one of them had Colonel Ian Cameron onboard.

She stepped out of her office and looked down at her secretary, who had a telephone to her ear. Jamilla looked up at her boss and shook her head.

"Nothing. It just says his cell is switched off."

"Keep trying, honey."

"Will do, Boss."

At twelve noon Oddhouse himself phoned from the top floor.

"Mini, darling, how goes it with your barbarian from the CIA? We want him working on part two yesterday at the latest."

"Rupe, he was supposed to be here at eleven. I've had Jamilla calling his cell every ten minutes for the last hour, and to make it worse his brother phoned saying he didn't go home last night."

"Shit!" And then, "This is either a blessing or a damned disaster. Have you called the cops?"

"No..."

"Well call them, for goodness's sake! If somebody has killed him..." There was a thrill in his voice. "Do you know what that would do for sales? We get a ghost to write his unfinished autobiography—no pun intended—*To Live by the Sword*! No, no—*To Live and Die by the Sword*!"

"Rupert, you can't sack me, can you?"

"Not really, why?"

"Then go screw yourself!"

"Call the cops!"

"No, I'm going to call someone else. Leave it to me."

She hung up and called a Washington DC number. It rang once and an efficient, female voice answered, "This is the office of Senator Walther Gannett, how may I help you?"

"Tell Walther it's Araminta and I need to talk to him right now. It's urgent!"

"Hold the line please, Ms Whitley." There was a moment's silence and then the well-groomed voice of Senator Walther Gannett came on the line.

"Mini, sweetheart, have you finally decided to publish my autobiography?"

"I'm waiting till you become president or, better still, notorious. Walt. Listen, are you still involved in national security committees and all that crap you dabble in?"

"That's why you sleep secure in your bed at night, baby."

"Sure, it has nothing to do with my two Rottweilers. Who was that guy you told me about at George's dinner party at The Chapel? You said he was a genius and ran some kind of outfit that was above top secret and you couldn't tell me about it, only you were trying to get me to hit the sack with you...? You remember?"

"Oh, yeah. I shouldn't have done that. You should try to forget, Mini. They just call him Nero. Apparently he once burned down a restaurant or a hotel or something because the chef made him mad. The caviar was not beluga or it was two degrees too cold or something. But he won't write an autobiography for you."

"That's not what I want. I need to talk to him."

"You can't just talk to Nero, honey. I'm not sure he really even exists."

"You talk to him."

"Well, yeah, I know how to..."

"Listen, tell him Colonel Ian Cameron has disappeared. If you get me an interview with him, I'll get you a ghost-writer and we'll publish your autobiography."

"You serious? I mean, are you serious that Cameron has disappeared?"

"I am serious."

"Are you going ahead with publication?"

"Of course!"

"Of course, right. OK, I'll talk to someone. I'll do my best, but I can't guarantee anything. Like I said, he doesn't really exist."

She hung up and immediately called Jamilla.

"Still nothing, Boss."

"OK, leave it, start calling around all the hospitals."

She didn't wait for a reply. She hung up, went to her desk and tried to keep busy. She kept telling herself Cameron was a rogue and he'd probably got drunk and gone back with some dame to her place and he would call in the next few minutes, or an hour. But she knew from the hollow feeling she had in her gut that she was kidding herself. That just wasn't Ian's style. Underneath his devil-may-care exterior, he was serious, punctual and efficient.

At one PM Jamilla came in to say there was no record of a Colonel James Cameron having been admitted to a hospital in New York last night or this morning.

At two o'clock her telephone rang. The screen told her the number was not known. She tried to remain cool and answered, "This is Araminta Whitely,"

"Miss Whitley, you asked your friend, Senator Walther Gannett to pull strings and arrange for me to call you."

"Oh, are you..."

"I am. I must tell you that it is unheard of for me to make such a call and I have severely reprimanded the senator. This telephone call is not happening and will not show on any records. Are we clear?"

"Oh, yes, I am sorry..."

"There is no need for you to apologize. You did not compel me to telephone, I undertook to do so of my own free will. You are publishing a book by Colonel Ian Cameron."

"That's correct. Yes, I am."

"*Sex, Drugs and Rock 'n' Roll at the White House.*"

"That's the one."

"A suitably sordid, vulgar title for a sordid, vulgar work. It names names, as the saying goes. And he has now disappeared."

She filled him in as to the details, then added, "Walther said you were a genius and a rare man of honor in a world of rats."

"Indeed?"

"I mean, if he had been assassinated, it would do wonders for sales, but I like Ian, and I'd hate for anything to happen to him."

"Quite. It is usually preferable to avoid assassination. Not always, but usually. In this case it would tend to confirm his allegations and would thus be avoided. I will send somebody to talk to you. They'll be in touch. Good day, Miss Whitley."

He had hung up before she could answer and she was left with the peculiar sensation of not being sure if the phone call had happened at all.

At ODIN HEADQUARTERS on Wilson Avenue, in Arlington, Nero pressed a button and disconnected the call to Oddhouse Publishing. He pursed his lips a moment and raised his eyes to look at me. "Why," he asked, "do people who shouldn't keep writing memoirs they oughtn't? It is an epidemic."

I said, "Am I going to New York?"

"I don't know. Colonel Ian Cameron is not a lovable scoundrel, Alex. He is a monster. It is possible..." He trailed off and dialed a number. It rang a couple of times and one of those English, clipped, stiff-upper-lip voices answered.

"Nero, what can I do for you?"

"Brigadier, you are familiar with the name Colonel Ian Cameron."

"I am."

"Is he on one of your lists?"

"If he's not he should be, but we are curious about this book he's about to publish. Why do you ask?"

"Somebody may have beaten you to the punch. Last night he disappeared. It was not one of your operatives?"

"No. With a bit of luck he'll have drunk himself to death in some dive in a backstreet somewhere."

Nero thrust out his lower lip. "Perhaps, but it seems to me there may be people who want him dispatched at the moment, or at least punished, *pour encourager les autres*. Some of them could be people of interest to us."

"Well, good luck. If you need anything, give us a shout."

He disconnected the call. "Alex,"

"Yes, sir."

"Go to New York, speak to Miss Araminta Whitley, find out what has happened to the colonel, who has done it and for what reason. This may afford us an opportunity to rip up a few ugly weeds from our garden. Allegations in books can be refuted and denied, but if somebody has panicked and resorted to murder, then perhaps we can catch them *sanguis in manibus!*"

I stood. "You know me, there is nothing I like better than a bit of *sanguis in manibus*. I'll call you when I get there."

"There is no need for that." He reached for a file, opened it and started reading. "Call me when you have something."

"As long as you're OK." I opened the door. "I wouldn't want you worrying about me or anything."

"That will be fine," he said, and dismissed me with his fingertips.

I paused in Lovelock's office, ostensibly to ask her about booking me a flight to New York. Lovelock is five-foot eleven in her bare feet, her skin is purple-black, her eyes are enormous and almond-shaped, and she has the kind of curves that cause men to walk into lampposts. Not only that, she moves with the grace of a panther and her voice is like hot chocolate laced with an especially fine whiskey.

"You want to book me a flight to New York, Lovelock?"

"When for?" She asked it like it was really immoral and she enjoyed it.

"I have to be there today. You want to come with me? I know a place we could dine..."

She leaned forward with her chin on her hands and her fingers framing her perfect face. She smiled. "Oh, Alex, I would *love* that. I'll get my husband to pick us up in half an hour."

"You're cruel, Lovelock. Cruel."

"Poor Alex. But you know what? By the time I book it, you get to the airport, check in...you may as well drive. Four hours. The way you drive, maybe three and a half." I made for the door. She called, "I'll book you in at the Plaza. They have *really* comfy beds."

Lovelock wasn't wrong. It was a chance to put my new Factory Five, 450 bhp Shelby Cobra through its paces, and I made it in three hours and forty-five minutes; and by the time I got there I wanted to do it all over again. Instead I headed for the south end of the park, four blocks past Columbus Circle on Broadway, and managed to squeeze into a space outside Citibank.

Through the revolving glass and steel doors in Oddhouse Plaza, I crossed the gleaming marble lobby and let one of the five elevators take me to the sixteenth floor. When I stepped out of the sliding doors I was in another lobby. This one looked like it was made of polished toffee. Even the reception desk was made of amber marble, with a logo of an open book with a pop-up crooked house emerging from it. I figured it was a hangover from the early days when the company published only children's books. Today it was one of the biggest corporations on the planet.

The girl behind the desk had a frilly lace blouse, a string of pearls around her neck, a dark bun behind her neck and pretty dark eyes. I told her, "I'm here to see Araminta Whitley. She's expecting me but she doesn't know my name."

She smiled and squinted and cocked her head on one side. I said, "Tell her it's Alex Mason, from DC."

"Comics?"

"The city where the president lives. Washington."

"Oh," she buzzed and singsonged, "Ms. Whitley, I have a Mr. Alex Mason here for you from Washington DC." She pressed a button and smiled at me. "You were right. She was expecting you, and she didn't know your name."

She told me where the door was and a moment later I knocked and entered. It was a large, corner office. The walls were lined with bookcases and where there were no books, the walls held framed book covers. Her desk was littered with manuscripts and she, a handsome woman in her mid-forties, was striding across the floor to meet me with both hands reaching for mine.

"Mr. Mason? Alex? May I call you Alex? I'm Araminta." She grasped my hand and didn't so much shake it as squeeze it. "This has been one of the—no, scrub that, it *has* been *the* longest day of my *life!* Thank you so much for coming. Will you sit?"

She took rapid steps to adjust a chair at her desk. Then stopped and turned.

"You are... You said Washington, I mean..."

I smiled. "Nero sent me to talk to you about Colonel Ian Cameron. I am the man you were expecting."

She sighed and sagged, like the repressed sigh was the only thing keeping her upright. "Thank God."

I sat in the chair and frowned at her.

"We are going to need to go over this in baby steps, Araminta. I need to know what made you call Nero," I smiled and raised my eyebrows, "and how you knew *how* to call Nero, why you thought this would be of interest to him, and, when we've gone through that, I need you to tell me in minute detail exactly what happened."

She leaned her ass against the desk and crossed her arms. She eyed me a moment, then started to speak.

"You probably don't know this. Most people don't. But, publishing houses, especially big corporate publishing houses like Oddhouse, wield a lot more power than you might expect. We pull a lot of strings behind the scenes. You'd be amazed at how seriously the 'powers that be,'" she made little quote signs with her fingers, "take the whole issue of what books get published and become major bestsellers each year—and which ones don't. I was told not so long ago by a recent president that Hollywood and the major publishing houses are the most powerful tools in social engineering that Western Powers have at their disposal, more so even than Twitter, whatever Elon may think."

"I can believe that."

"So major editors like me, in major publishing houses like this, get invited to events, parties and dinners where they rub shoulders with very powerful people who sometimes get drunk. I was at a party a while back at a Texas ranch which shall remain nameless, and Senator Walther Gannett was there. He got drunk and started talking about a man he had met during a briefing to a Senate Committee on national security. The man was vast, rude, terrifyingly intelligent and insufferably arrogant and blunt. His name was Nero— nothing else—and nobody at the briefing knew what department he was attached to, but they all knew he was probably the most powerful, dangerous man in the room."

I made a mental note to have Senator Gannett

kneecapped in the near future and started to ask, "So what made you..."

"Quite aside from the fact that he sounded fascinating, if you knew how much is riding on this novel, if you knew the shock waves that will rock through DC when this hits the newsstands, you would realize that, the moment I understood that something had happened to Ian, I *knew* that I needed somebody very special to look for him and help him."

"So you called your friend Senator Gannett."

"Exactly."

"Ms. Whitley, Araminta, Nero is a sort of code name for the man who is the head of the Office of the Director of Intelligence Networks. He deals with threats from Russia, China, North Korea, Middle Eastern conflicts..." I smiled. "You can't call him because your cat got stuck up a tree, or even if one of your writers has gone missing."

Her cheeks flushed. "Oh, now don't I feel foolish?" But after a moment her blue eyes went hard and she said, "And yet, here you are."

"And yet, here I am, like Jack Nicholson in the *Witches of Eastwick*. I'm here because we do happen to have an interest in Colonel Cameron."

"I bet you have. Maybe some of you are in his book."

The comment annoyed me more than it should have. I smiled without humor. "I doubt it, and as a courtesy I'll refrain from speculating about your private life or assuming you snort coke with champagne-drinking glitteratti." I gave a small shrug. "Given, you know, that stereotypes are anathema and I know nothing about you; and," I added with heavy meaning, "that I am about to ask for your help."

She flushed again and raised her eyebrows. "I'll consider myself told off—for the second time in five minutes! Maybe I should sit down and we can start over."

She moved around the desk and as she sat I asked her, "When was the last time you saw the colonel?"

"Last night. We are celebrating an extended book launch with several events at hotels, major bookstores and other venues. This one was at the Plaza. The great and the good from New York society and the media were there, TV, the press, we even had a Hollywood producer who was interested in the film rights. After dinner Ian got up and gave a talk. He's amazing." She shook her head. "He is a natural showman. Fascinating. He had everybody mesmerized. The man is a goose who will never stop laying golden eggs. I pray that nothing has happened to him."

"Did anything happen during the talk?"

"Nothing special. He made everybody laugh…"

"So how about after the talk? What happened then?"

She shrugged. "He was restless, said he was going to take a walk and smoke a cigarette, maybe have a drink somewhere. I made him promise to be here by eleven this morning, but he never showed up."

"I assume he's usually punctual."

"Very. He's a military man. Discipline is everything. Also his phone has been unobtainable all day. His brother, Alasdair, called me this morning and said he hadn't gone home last night. Apparently, since he's been back in New York he's been very particular about telling his brother where he is and where he is going to be. Alasdair promised to let me know as soon as he showed up, but so far I've heard nothing. Obviously my secretary has phoned around to all the hospitals, but we've drawn a blank. He has vanished off the face of the Earth."

"Obviously you haven't called the cops."

She grinned. "No, I called the Office of the Director of Intelligence Networks instead."

She invited me to smile with her, but I was still sore at her crack about being in the book, so I just narrowed my eyes and looked at the window. Then I told her, "I am going to need a copy of the book. I'll give you a receipt and I'll sign a nondisclosure agreement."

She buzzed her secretary and made arrangements. When she'd finished I said, "I'm almost done, Araminta. I'll get the details from the book. But I have a couple of questions. First, realistically, how much damage is this book going to do, and to what extent can he back it up with proof?"

"Simple answers—a *lot* of damage to some very highly placed people. There will be sackings among senior officials and resignations from both Houses, and from the judiciary. And you can be damn sure there will be resignations. The FBI are going to have a field day. And there will be a public outcry, because this will be a national embarrassment. And proof? Total. I've seen the evidence. He can prove every word."

I nodded. "OK, he must have had a mentor at the CIA, his handler, godfather..."

"Yeah, he names him in the book. General Mike Ustinov. He used to be senator for Texas, he was the chairman of the Committee on Border Control, and a vocal supporter of Trump's wall. He was also governor of Texas for several years, as well as director of the CIA. He has quite a résumé."

"OK." I nodded a few times, thinking. "I'll have to make

some inquiries. I'll get back to you within the next few hours."

Fifteen minutes later, with an advance copy of the colonel's book in my possession, I rose and made my way to the door. With my hand on the handle I stopped and turned to look back at her. She was staring at me and frowning. I said:

"By the way, Ms. Whitley, the Office of the Director of Intelligence Networks you mentioned earlier?" I said, "It doesn't exist."

Scan the QR code below to purchase ALL THE KING'S MEN.
Or go to: righthouse.com/all-the-kings-men

# NOTES

## CHAPTER 1

1. See *Executive Order*

## CHAPTER 4

1. See *Executive Order*